The Planck Factor

Also by Debbi Mack

Identity Crisis

Least Wanted

Riptide

Deep Six

Invisible Me

The Planck Factor

Debbi Mack

Renegade Press

Savage, MD

Renegade Press
P.O. Box 156
Savage, MD

This is a work of fiction. Any resemblance to actual events or persons living or dead is entirely coincidental.

Library of Congress Cataloging-in-Publication Data
The Planck Factor by Debbi Mack
ISBN: 978-0-9906985-5-5
Library of Congress Control Number: 2016951288

DEDICATION

For Nancy Mack and Ken MacClune

"Suppose powerful accelerators managed to produce large numbers of Planck mass particles and that somehow a bomb was made with them. According to our theory, such a bomb would release exactly half the energy released by a conventional nuclear weapon with the same overall mass. In other words, such an expensive quantum gravitational weapon would be precisely half as powerful as a much cheaper conventional nuclear weapon. For more massive particles (say with masses equal to two or three times the Planck mass), the result would be even worse. I was pleased to find that even generals would probably not be dumb enough to hire Lee or me."*

*Unfortunately, the possibility that $E\rho$ might be negative reverses this argument, as explained in our paper.

João Magueijo, Faster Than the Speed of Light (Perseus Publishing, 2003), pp. 252-253.

PROLOGUE

KEVIN

He knew he had to act. Major plans were in the works. And lives were on the line.

But he had to eliminate Fred.

Fred had joined the group, ostensibly as a card-carrying anti-government dissident. But something felt off about him.

Fred wasn't genuinely involved. Kevin had always figured he was up to no good.

It was increasingly clear his allegiance belonged to the woman—a novelist, no less—who was using information he'd learned by infiltrating the group.

In short, Fred was a spy. Kevin shuddered, feeling he'd had an epiphany. This was entirely the wrong time for a spy to come along and botch the group's plans.

His only option was to kill Fred.

CHAPTER ONE

JESSICA

"This sucks!" I shook my head. Why did I open the story with a man, alone at night on a twisty mountain road? I may as well have written, "It was a dark and stormy night . . . ." I sighed and reconsidered the first lines again.

I had reworked the opening scene of my novel more than a few times. How many ways were there to show that danger lay ahead?

I banged out a few more lines, but they still didn't seem quite right. Sometimes writing was like turning on a faucet. I could sit at the keyboard and the words would flow nonstop, brain to fingertips. On days like that, I couldn't type fast enough. This was not one of those days.

"Ugh!" I stopped typing and read (for the third time? or was it the fourth?) the intro to my suspense novel-in-progress, *The Planck Factor*, and again reviewed the other scenarios under which Daniel could be killed. I'd chosen an auto accident along a mountain road—plausible enough, but overdone. Would an editor scan the first few lines, roll her eyes, and toss the manuscript into the round file?

How about a mountain road in broad daylight? Nice sunny day. Totally defying expectations. Almost Hitchcock-ian. But the night scenario was so evocative. I liked the dark and the fog, the feeling of dread, the promise of malevolence to come. It was an old trick but, in this case, maybe a good trick.

I envisioned other possibilities—Daniel pushed from a window and made to look like he had fallen? No, no—that and other kinds of accidental death would leave a very obvious body. In my version, Daniel was burned beyond recognition. Only dental records could establish that the body was his. I liked that.

Wait! What if Daniel were attacked in his lab? Then what if someone set it on fire and made it look like an accident? He could be working alone, hear a noise, and think Swede was coming. Then—wham! He's knocked unconscious or killed. And the poor schmuck gets roasted.

I breathed a deep sigh. If I went that way, I'd have to rethink the whole thing. And that dark scene on the road was so clear in my mind.

I rubbed my eyes, sipped some coffee, and gazed out the window of my condo at the stellar view of the Flatirons, the rocky protrusions thrusting upward at the western edge of Boulder, Colorado. They glowed rust-red in the sunrise.

After a five-minute break, I returned to the keyboard. Working on another scene might help. And I needed to develop the character Alexis.

φφφ

After an hour's work, I looked over the results. Not bad. Might even work—assuming it wasn't too detailed. I thought of Elmore Leonard's advice: "Leave out the boring parts." What the heck? Run the changes by my writers group. See what they think.

The sun had risen and the Flatirons stood in sharp relief against a bright blue sky, the white-capped peaks of the Rockies poking up in the distance. I stood and stretched my arms overhead. "Time to make the doughnuts."

I finished my coffee, washed out the cup and my French press, and gathered my belongings before heading off for a meeting with my program adviser. We had a friendly ongoing argument, of sorts. I initially wanted to write my master's thesis on how genre fiction could have literary value. She convinced me to choose another subject. But then she challenged me to write a novel. I took her up on that and even joined the writers group.

As I placed my belongings into my old Dodge Dart, I thought about how genre fiction was often equally worthy of the acclaim often granted to so-called "literary" works. I had no idea if I could accomplish such a thing. I told myself, "You're not trying to write *War and Peace*. Just write a story you would read." What I'd settled on was a suspense story with a hint of science fiction and touch of espionage at its heart. Writing about a scientific topic was a bit of a stretch, but a good one, I hoped. Plus my research into physics was fascinating.

I started the car and headed toward the university.

As I drove off, I glanced in my rearview mirror. Two men in tan jumpsuits emerged from a dark van sitting in my parking lot. A young man with flaming red hair carrying a large case and an older man with a clipboard. They seemed to be walking toward my building.

A dark van? Just like in my story? Too weird. I shook my head and laughed. *Jessica Evans, you're getting paranoid. Since when did life really imitate art?*

CHAPTER TWO

DANIEL

Daniel had thought about burning the evidence of the research he and Swede had worked so hard to gather-- but throwing away all those years of work was more than he could bear. Did it come down to pride? Daniel maneuvered his VW bug along the switchback turns. Was it foolish pride that had led Robert Oppenheimer to head up the Manhattan Project?

Not pride--fear. Fear that Nazi Germany would develop the atom bomb first. Today, we're not fighting Nazis. Today, it's much harder to figure out who the bad guys are.

The VW's headlights pierced the light veil of fog descending along Oregon's coastal range. In places, the veil thickened into a shroud. The headlight beams swept across sentinel trunks of tall Douglas firs. Daniel squinted from the reflected glare as the car plunged into another cottony patch of fog.

All the things he'd never told Alexis and the arrangements he had made in case the worst should happen. He'd done his best to keep Alexis out of it and protect himself. Found someone who didn't have as big a stake in the whole thing as he and Swede did. Someone other than Alexis that he could trust.

A wave of guilt over what he'd never said to Alexis mingled with his anxiety about where all his work could lead if allowed to get into the wrong hands.

Daniel turned the wheel hard to follow a tight curve, and the VW slid sideways beneath him--a feeling of being totally out of control--in keeping with the rest of his life.

He steered as far from the precipitous drop along the roadside as he could. One moment, Daniel peered through the murk. The next, he squinted as his rearview mirror reflected the glare of high beams.

Daniel's heartbeat quickened. *Keep calm*, he told himself. Then, the car jolted as the vehicle behind him rammed his car.

"What the fuck?" he said. Daniel gripped the wheel harder. He focused on breathing evenly and staying on the road.

Daniel spotted a crossroad up ahead that led into the mountains. If he could just turn fast enough, maybe the vehicle behind him would overshoot the road. Hopefully, he'd lose the tail.

As he approached the road, Daniel waited until the last second and yanked the wheel left. The car spun as if floating. Daniel held fast to the wheel. A loud crash filled the air. Everything went dark.

φφφ

ALEXIS

Two weeks. That's all the time Alexis had allowed herself after her fiancé, Daniel's, tragic death. Just two weeks off. Then it was back to her studies. She had a limited scholarship, after all. No parents, no big inheritance, no trust fund to rely on. She couldn't drop out of school after all the work she'd done on her master's thesis on existentialism and modern literature. She had to keep going.

Alexis had to stay on track to get her master's in philosophy at the University of Oregon within the three years her scholarship allowed. But now her studies were more than a means to a scholastic end. Her textbooks were a blanket wrapped around her consciousness. One that protected her from the death of her parents barely a year ago, under circumstances too painful to contemplate. And now Daniel. It was too much to take in.

Alexis worked in her carrel until the lights flickered. The library would be closing in ten minutes. Nine o'clock already? Where did the time go?

Reluctantly, she closed out her word processing program and turned off her laptop. She placed her books neatly to one side on the carrel's shelf and the little paper placard that read "Reserved" in the middle.

Alexis placed her belongings in a knapsack and, with a casual wave to the reference librarian at the desk, strolled out the door toward the parking lot. She dropped the knapsack onto the passenger seat of her aging Toyota Tercel, rounded the car, and got in.

As her Tercel roared to life, farther back in the lot, a small dark van's engine did the same. The van held three men--one behind the wheel and two in the back. Alexis eased out of the space and exited the lot. The van followed.

CHAPTER THREE

JESSICA

My adviser Shelley removed her glasses and set them on the desk. "You're making progress with your thesis. I must say I'm impressed." She ran her fingers through her shoulder-length hair and rolled her head back, rotating it as if to loosen her neck muscles.

I could feel an inadvertent smile form as I pulled my manuscript pages from a folder. "If you like that, I think you're going to love this."

Shelley put her glasses back on and glanced at the first page. Laughing soundlessly, she grinned. "Oh, my God. You're actually writing that novel?"

"How could I not accept such a challenge?"

She turned her attention to the story. After turning the page, she said, "Well, you're off to a rousing start, that's for sure."

"And you don't think the beginning is too corny?"

"Well." Shelley paused and set aside the manuscript. "It's not exactly *War and Peace*, is it?"

"Exactly! I'm not trying to write the Great American Novel. I'm just trying to tell a great story."

Shelley shrugged. "To me, it reads like the stuff that sells. Not that I'm a big expert."

"Nobody is."

Shelley nodded. "Got that right. Look how that 'Fifty Shades' book did. Who would have thought?" She shook her head. "Think you can keep this up while working on your thesis? Writing a novel isn't the easiest thing."

"I know, I know. I've been working on it slowly over time. Almost done, actually. I'm just going over it again to make sure it doesn't completely stink."

"Well, okay." She delivered a probing gaze. "Just don't let it interfere with your *real* work here."

"I won't," I said. "Promise."

"Uh huh," she replied. She pointed two fingers toward her eyes, then at me. "Don't forget."

She picked up the manuscript again. "Who knows? With some real effort, you might even prove your original point." She scanned the pages.

That was as close to a concession as I would ever get from Shelley.

"This almost reads like a movie script," she added. "All high concept and big action and suspense. Not that it's bad. But if you can make it more than just that, you could make it amazing."

φφφ

Later, I drove home after a long day at the library, followed by a shift at the bookstore. It was almost nine. I was beat and starved. Lunch had been a cup of yogurt and a banana. More like an appetizer than a meal. As I'd shelved books, my thoughts had been so consumed with the story, half the customers who asked me questions were treated to a dazed look and the cogent response, "Huh?"

Show, don't tell. Weave in backstory. Truisms, guides, rules, pointers—call them what you will. It was the kind of stuff writers heard all the time. Yet, somehow, writers were always bending these rules just a bit. Bending them to serve their own purpose. Inserting huge chunks of backstory so colorful you didn't mind reading it—even though conventional wisdom said to do so would slow the narrative. And adverbs. Never use an adverb. Oh, really? Well, I wish I had a dime for every adverb I'd read, even in the best-written books. Never say never.

After parking in front of my building, I grabbed my shoulder bag and knapsack and hiked the stairs to my condo. Despite my skimpy lunch, I cringed at the thought of making dinner. Maybe I'd scramble a couple of eggs. Order take-out Thai.

I was starved but too tired to even think of what to eat and whether to make it myself or leave the cooking to someone else.

I tossed my shoulder bag onto the couch and the manuscript onto a pile of waste paper. I used the blank sides to print drafts: waste not, want not—and I couldn't afford to waste anything. Take-out would be nice, but expensive. The scrambled eggs were sounding better all the time. I figured I'd do some writing, then decide.

I sat at my desk and turned on the computer. Simply watching it boot up gave me a vague feeling of dread. Opening the word processing program would only increase my anxiety. Here we go again, I thought. How many times do I have to review this? How many iterations of the same thing must I churn out before it's perfect? As perfect as I'll ever get it, anyway.

I took a deep breath and began to work.

φφφ

ALEXIS

Alexis arrived home and hauled her laptop and files up to her apartment. She was just putting the key in the lock when she thought she heard someone whisper her name.

The whisper came from the darkened landing above her, making her whirl with such force she almost dropped everything. She peered into the gloom but saw nothing. Eugene, Oregon, was a small and relatively safe town, but no place was completely safe, was it?

Her hand trembling, she quickly turned the deadbolt and reinserted the key to turn the knob.

"Alexis."

She yipped in fear. This time, there was no mistaking it. Someone was up there.

As she turned the key and hurled herself against the door to get in, the voice said, louder and closer now, "Alexis, it's just me. It's Swede."

Alexis gaped at the tall figure looming above her on the stairs. "Jesus Christ," she said. "What the hell are you doing, Swede? You scared the shit out of me."

Swede drew close and said, "Let me in. Quick. We need to talk."

Alexis backed inside, and the tall, dark-haired man followed. He closed the door, turning and leaning against it, as if someone were on the other side threatening to break it down. Swede was breathing hard, his eyes closed.

How Alan Sweetser got a nickname like Swede was anyone's guess. He might be many things, Alexis thought, but Swedish wasn't one of them.

"What in God's name are you doing here?" She got a good look at him and her voice softened a bit. "What's wrong? Jeez, you look like hell."

Swede brushed curly, dark locks back from a pale forehead shining with perspiration. He took a shuddering breath, opened his eyes--a startling lucid green--and said, "Someone followed you here. They . . . I think they're after something. It may relate to Daniel's research. Our research, that is."

Alexis, who'd been gaping in astonishment, laughed--a sound as harsh as ripping fabric.

"What the hell would I know about your research?" she said, making it sound like an accusation. Poking a finger into Swede's chest, she hissed, "You two were thick as fucking thieves about what you were doing. Daniel never discussed your precious research with me. Would've thought you guys worked for the CIA, from what little either of you told me about it. And you, of all people, know that goddamned good and well!" Her voice had climbed to a wail by the time she reached the end of her speech. A fleeting memory of Daniel's face brought grief bubbling to the surface of her consciousness. First one tear, then several others. The next thing Alexis knew, she was sobbing, over all the wasted time, the meaningless arguments, the wedge that research had driven between Daniel and her.

"Oh, God," Her voice shook from the force of her sobs. "Daniel. Oh . . . shit."

She swatted the tears away, swiping a backhand across her runny nose, and glared at Swede. "What the hell do you want?" she muttered through clenched teeth.

Swede gulped. "The research. I thought he might have . . . told you . . . . "

"Goddamn it, Swede!" Alexis paused, hunting for the words. "So what are you saying? You think Daniel went back on his word and spilled his guts during pillow talk? Well, surprise! He didn't, okay? He never told me a thing. All the secrecy was no joy to live with, let me tell you. I knew something was troubling him, but if I tried to discuss it-- whoops!--we couldn't because it had to do with his research. There were nights not long before the accident when he couldn't sleep. He'd get up and pace, so I'd ask if he was okay. And he was like, 'Sure, sure. I'm fine.' But he wasn't fine and he

wasn't telling me about it because it was all
connected to that research, wasn't it?"

She paused, her ragged breathing matched only by
Swede's, and said, "Now you have the fucking gall to
come here and act like I'm supposed to know something
about this goddamned mystery research that was
wrecking our lives, when you know Daniel wouldn't
have told me and you know I know nothing about it."
She paused again and swallowed, trying to regain
self-control. "So why don't you just get the hell out
of here?"

"You may not know what Daniel was doing," Swede
stammered, "but they don't know that."

"Who the hell is--"

Then someone pounded on the door.

φφφ

JESSICA

After spending the better part of an hour going over Swede's
introduction to the story, I stopped and considered the result.
Getting there, I thought. But how can I really know if it's there?

As I went about fixing my scrambled-egg dinner, my cell
phone rang. I flipped it open. (I won't buy a "smart" phone.
Too pricey.) Private caller. For the third time that week. I don't
like to take calls unless I recognize the number. I sighed and
ignored it. I was melting butter in the pan when it rang again.
Private caller. Hmm . . . could it be that editor I met at the
symposium two weeks ago? But why didn't she leave a message?
I took the call to find out.

"Jessica Evans?" I couldn't place the voice—deep and
androgynous—although it had a familiar ring.

"Yes?"

"Look out your window but don't move the blinds or make
it obvious." A brief pause. "Someone is watching you."

CHAPTER FOUR

JESSICA

"Who is this?" I said. My chest tightened and my pulse raced.

"Look for a dark van. Down a few spaces to your right. Remember, don't—"

I snapped the phone shut. *What the fuck?* My pulse was pounding now. I thought of the story. The dark van in the parking lot that morning. And Alexis being followed by a dark van. Too weird. But it had to be a coincidence. Just some wacko.

The phone rang again. I jumped at the sound. Private caller again. I set the phone on the counter and moved back, staring at it as if it were about to explode.

The phone stopped ringing but started again within seconds. A burning odor filled the air. For a crazy moment, I thought it was the phone. Then I saw smoke billowing from the pan.

"Goddamn it!"

I turned off the burner and set the pan aside, surveying the wreckage within it, the butter singed on its surface in shades of mottled black and brown.

"Great," I said. "Just great."

The phone stopped ringing, then started again almost immediately.

I snatched it up, checked the number. Private caller. Well, Private Caller was about to get a piece of my mind.

"Jessica?" It was the voice. "Have you looked out the window?"

"No. No, I haven't looked out the damn window. I've been too busy trying to burn my place down."

Silence. "Jessica—"

"No, listen up. I'm trying to make dinner and just ruined my best pan—thanks to you. So why don't you leave me alone. Quit fucking with my head."

"The van—"

"Fuck the van and fuck you. And how do you know there's a van outside my place? Unless, of course, you're in it. I'm calling the cops. Right . . . now!"

I hit the button to disconnect and immediately dialed 911. In the few seconds it took for them to answer, I turned off the light and edged up to the window so I could peek through the crack in the blinds without moving them.

Among the vehicles in the lot, I saw a dark van. Looked like the same van I'd seen that morning. My stomach felt hollow, as if I were plunging down a skyscraper in a fast-moving elevator. What was going on? I thought again about the story, but no one knew the details except my writers group. And none of them would play a sick joke like this.

"911. What is the nature of your emergency?"

"Um. I've been getting strange calls." My voice sounded strangled. "And there's this van parked outside my place." I groped for the right words, but they all sounded crazy.

"Threatening calls?"

"Not exactly. Just . . . strange."

"Ma'am, this is an emergency line. If someone is trying to hurt you or break into your house—"

"No, no. And I'm in a condo." My voice shook. "But this person called and said I was being watched by someone in a dark van. And there's a dark van, just sitting there."

"I'm sorry, ma'am, but there's no law against someone parking in a public place. And, just so I'm clear, did you say the caller threatened you?"

"No," I mumbled. "Never mind."

I couldn't even hit *67 to trace the call. The private caller ID meant the number was blocked.

I closed the phone and, forgetting my hunger, decided to ignore the van and resumed my work.

φφφ

JOE

"What now, Chief?"

The question came from Billy, a 25-year-old, red-haired freckled fellow, new to the game and full of himself, in Cotter's opinion. From where he squatted on a small stool in the back of the van, the kid grinned at Cotter.

Cotter looked at Billy. "Keep tabs on her phone."

"But I think we been made."

"Did I ask what you thought?"

Billy frowned and turned back to the blinking console.

After several moments of protracted silence, Billy said, "You had the goggles, Chief. You could see that Evans chick as good as me."

Cotter took a deep breath, as if inhaling the fresh air of a new day.

"It doesn't really matter," he said.

Billy grunted. "I just hope she don't run."

"What if she does?"

"Complicates things, huh?"

Cotter shrugged. "She runs, we follow. Simple as that."

Billy snorted. "Oh, yeah."

"By the way, Billy?"

"Uh huh?"

"Don't call me 'Chief.' Understand, Sport?"

φφφ

ALEXIS

Swede leapt away from the door and stared at it. Another round of pounding ensued.

"Young lady, I know you're in there!" An indignant voice from the other side.

With an exasperated sigh, Alexis checked the peephole. It was her upstairs neighbor, a white-haired old man named Klaus who often complained in a strident Teutonic accent about her music being too loud.

"It's just the asshole from upstairs," she muttered to Swede, who kept eyeing the door as if a troll lurked behind it.

Yet another series of jarring knocks. Finally, Klaus harrumphed and said, "I know you're in there. They could hear you yelling a mile away. Keep it down or I'll call the police."

Muffled muttering followed as Klaus turned to go back upstairs. Through the peephole, Alexis watched him leave, then turned to Swede, folding her arms across her chest.

"That was fun. What shall we do next?"

"Alexis." Swede took a deep breath and held his hands out in a placating gesture. "Please believe me when I tell you this. You have to leave here. We both have to go."

Alexis shook her head. "Go? Go where? I'm not going anywhere with you." Her voice trailed off. "Daniel's dead, Swede. And you and me, we died long before that. Let's not go there again."

Swede threw up his hands. "I'm not trying to get back together, if that's what you think."

"Good," Alexis said. She had cared for Swede. Maybe even loved him. But his brooding and pessimism could really get to her. Bright, but unstable. That was an apt description of Alan Sweetser. When they were together, at times, he would simply shut her out. When their differences finally tore Swede and Alexis apart, she turned to their mutual friend, Daniel. He was more patient, more even-tempered, and their relationship grew beyond friendship. Swede accepted the situation with more grace than Alexis had thought him capable of. But she'd continued to sense weird vibes when Swede was around. Like the air before lightning strikes. So she tried to avoid having him around.

"At the risk of repeating myself," Swede said, "you need to get out of here."

"Why? I have no idea what you're talking about. And you never answered my question about who 'they' are."

Swede's brow furrowed. He looked almost ready to cry. "That's the thing. I don't know who they are. I just know that they're after our research. And if they get hold of it . . . ." He bowed his head and shook it as if dazed. "It will be very bad for all of us."

"Why?"

"Our discovery . . . ." Swede grimaced. "I . . . I can't tell you. I shouldn't. You're better off not knowing. Just in case . . . ."

"In case what?" It took all of Alexis' effort to keep from shouting.

Swede slumped. "In case they catch you. What you don't know, you can't tell them."

Alexis just stared, then started laughing.

Swede didn't smile. "You still don't get it."

"Don't get it? You came here to warn me about a bunch of strange somebody-or-others who are looking for information about your research, which you've already acknowledged I know nothing about." She spread her arms. "Hell, that's the best joke I've heard in ages. It's positively hysterical."

"I told you." Swede's voice took on an urgent tone. "They don't know that you don't know anything."

"Yes, and what I don't know, I can't tell them, right? I think we've been over this already."

Swede laid both hands on her shoulders and looked directly in her eyes. "That doesn't mean they won't try to make you talk."

Alexis' breath caught in her throat. "What do you mean?" She shuddered. "Jesus . . . you must be joking."

Swede grabbed her shoulders and looked straight at her. "Do I look like I'm joking?" he asked.

φφφ

JESSICA

When I checked again a half hour later, the van was still there. I could barely make out the vehicle's interior. Then I remembered Fred's binoculars. He'd left them here after our last hike through the woods. I ran for the closet and pulled them off the upper shelf. With the lights off, I took a chance that no one would notice if I moved the blinds just enough to get a clear view through the binoculars. I trained them on the van and saw . . . an empty interior.

Okay, so the front seat was empty. Someone could be in the back. Or the person who called me could just be crazy.

I continued to check on the van every fifteen minutes or so. It never moved. And I saw nothing to suggest it was occupied.

"This is nuts," I said.

As I stored the binoculars, it hit me that I still hadn't heard back from Fred Barkin. He had promised me information I needed to confirm a few details for the book. I dialed Fred's number. Went to voice mail. For the third time in two weeks. Weird.

"Hi, Fred. I'm calling again to try to set up a time to meet with you." I paused, not sure what else to say. "Just call when you get a chance, okay?"

A mutual friend introduced me to Fred after I'd explained that I needed advice from a geology expert. Fred was very helpful because he knew people and things that helped provide background for the book. After meeting to discuss some of the finer points I needed to cover, Fred asked if I would be interested in taking hikes with him in the foothills.

It was during these walks that I got to know Fred as a person. He was not only a geoscientist, but he was a nature lover, through and through.

A couple of weeks back, I got an email from Fred, insisting we meet to talk about something he'd learned. He'd said it was important and should be discussed face-to-face.

I picked up a paperweight Fred had given me the last time I saw him, after a camping trip he and a few friends took to Yellowstone. I shook the clear plastic half-globe, causing the snow to swirl against the backdrop of high peaks and green trees within it, a moose standing in the foreground.

"Since you couldn't come with us, I thought I'd get this for you," he'd said, blushing a bit. This small gesture seemed like the act of a little boy presenting an apple to the teacher. I told him I'd keep the ornament on my desk, and he'd seemed genuinely pleased.

I always felt like Fred had things on his mind but could never spit them out. I wondered what that was all about. Now, this business with the unreturned phone calls worried me. If something bad had happened, I expected that one of our friends would tell me. So why was he avoiding me?

I set the paperweight down and watched the snow slowly settle. It took my mind off the craziness with the van and the phone calls for a short while. But my thoughts turned back to them.

Forget it. It's ridiculous. Whoever called you is just nuts.

I had to relax, so I made myself a cup of herbal tea. I backed up my files onto an external hard drive and shut my computer off. Checked out the window again. The van was gone.

I exhaled. It felt like I'd been holding my breath for the past hour.

My hunger had returned with a vengeance, so I made some toast, gobbled it down and rinsed the plate and knife quickly, filling the scorched frying pan with soapy water and leaving it to soak overnight.

"I knew it was nuts," I muttered, padding off to get ready for bed.

CHAPTER FIVE

JESSICA

The next morning, I rose before dawn to take another crack at the story. I made a fresh pot of coffee in my French press and downed a quick bowl of Wheaties while checking email. Just for the hell of it, I peeked out the window again. Still no van. Good. I scrubbed out the pan in the sink and topped off my coffee before opening my word processing program.

φφφ

ALEXIS

Alexis couldn't believe she was going anywhere with Swede. She had sworn she would never talk to the man again, let alone travel with him.

I must be losing my mind.

But what he told her had scared her. Swede actually seemed to believe that her life was in danger from these people who were looking for the research he and Daniel had conducted. Research so secret and dangerous, he still wouldn't tell her about it.

Alexis stared out the passenger window of Swede's rented compact. She'd wanted to take her own car, but Swede was afraid they'd be followed. She had tossed a few bare necessities into a paper bag and, at Swede's insistence, disguised herself as best she could by wearing a hoodie, under which she tucked her hair. It had started to rain, providing the perfect excuse for Swede to dash for the car with his jacket over his head. He'd pulled the car up to the building, and Alexis had jumped in.

"I can't believe you brought a laptop," Swede said.

"I've been working too hard on this thesis to just leave it behind," Alexis snapped. In a forlorn voice, she added, "Who knows when I'll be able to go home again?"

Besides, maybe her experiences would add a new dimension to her thesis on existentialism. She giggled and shook her head.

"What's so funny?"

"Nothing." She waved a hand. "There's nothing funny about any of this."

Even so, she couldn't stop smirking. How ludicrous was this? Her dead fiancé's lab partner with whom she'd had a previous failed relationship was now whisking her away from some unidentified bad guys who were looking for research she knew nothing about. She snickered into her hand, in a desperate bid to stop herself.

"What?" Swede said.

"C'mon. Isn't this just the slightest bit absurd? Don't you feel the least bit . . . awkward?"

Swede's eyes darted between the rearview mirror, the road, and Alexis. "I probably would. If I weren't scared shitless."

CHAPTER SIX

JESSICA

I drained the last of my coffee, got up, and rinsed the cup. *Am I stretching this bit out too long?* At some point, Alexis has to insist on knowing what's going on. *Did I choose the right way to convince Swede to tell her?* Maybe I'd find the answers while taking a walk. The sun was coming up, and it looked like another beautiful day in Boulder. A nice day to work outdoors even.

I backed up my files, grabbed my shoulder bag and laptop— a nice lightweight model my parents had bought for me—and headed out the door.

Before leaving, I stopped to retrieve the previous day's mail. Probably nothing but bills, so I had put it off. Looked like nothing but junk—a blessing in its own small way.

As I sorted through the various flyers for stores where I wouldn't shop, coupon booklets for things I didn't need, catalogs for clothes I couldn't afford, and notifications of qualifying for major credit cards I never wanted, I came across a plain white envelope with no return address.

When I opened it, a sheet of white paper, folded in half, slid out. I unfolded it and read the printed message:

Be careful. You may be in danger.
A concerned friend.

φφφ

"And this person on the phone. You didn't recognize the voice?"

I nearly wept with frustration. How many times was the cop going to ask that?

"No! I didn't recognize the voice. Couldn't even tell you if it was male or female. They mentioned a van. It was there, then it was gone. Now, I've got this creepy anonymous note."

I paused, trying to calm down. The cop, a tall, skinny guy who looked about sixteen, gazed at me with eyes like blue glass, as devoid of expression as the rest of his face. A nameplate above his left breast pocket read "A.J. Montgomery."

"I wish I could help you," he said, waving the letter. "But this isn't a threat."

"But that phone call—"

"Yes, I understand. That is strange." His eyebrows rose, and the side of his mouth turned up in seeming acknowledgment. "I'm afraid I don't know what to tell you. Except keep a record of your calls and hang onto any other notes you get."

"Could you dust for fingerprints or something? Figure out if this guy—gal—whatever—is in your system?"

"I'm sorry. We can't ask the forensic lab to do that without some indication of a crime." He looked solemn. "Unless there's evidence of a genuine threat, we can't do anything."

My shoulders slumped. "So I'm right back where I started. Nowhere."

"Not really," Officer Montgomery said. "I'll file a report. Maybe we can't act on it now, but as I said, if you get more phone calls or notes like this, it might—and I want to emphasize *might*—establish a case for stalking."

"So I have to wait for something else to happen."

The cop nodded solemnly.

I sighed. "Goody."

φφφ

Instead of the park, I decided to head to The Cup on East Pearl Street, where I could work on the novel and drink socially responsible coffee at the same time. While I was at it, I'd treat myself to a turkey club sandwich. I could already taste the bacon, avocado, and Swiss cheese. Maybe I was being stalked by some loony, but I wasn't going to deny myself life's small pleasures.

I pondered the situation as I drove. Who could've written that note, and why? Then a bizarre scenario suggested itself. Could it have something to do with Fred's failure to return my phone calls? Or the thing he wanted to talk to me about? No way, I thought. It has to be a coincidence. Just my overactive imagination running away with me. Same for the note written by the anonymous caller. And what did the van have to do with anything?

Writing a novel hardly seemed like a dangerous occupation to me, but now I wasn't sure. Whatever the reason for my current problems, I felt glad to have taken all those free self-defense courses the university offered.

I parallel parked near Pearl Street, trying not to think about it. How much danger could I be in surrounded by people in downtown Boulder? The Cup seemed like a pretty good place to be.

Not that there was any shortage of good coffee shops in Boulder. The Cup was usually busy but not jammed to the gills with the regulars who hung out at Rocky Mountain Bookstore. Nor was it overrun with the earnest students in endless discussions of consciousness, the nature of time, and inter-dimensionality who favored the second-floor trappings of Java Joe's Café. Such conversation could be stimulating—to a point. Right now, I needed to focus on my story. Work out the details of what would happen next to Alexis and Swede.

I'll admit that I felt a smidgen of guilt for hanging out at The Cup, agonizing over the fate of fake people in a made-up situation instead of working on my thesis. But I was so eager to review this draft of my novel and put the final touches on it, I simply couldn't stop now.

I ordered my coffee and sandwich and then set up at a corner table to write.

CHAPTER SEVEN

They found a cheap motel well off the freeway, halfway to Portland. Swede peered out the window between the closed curtains, while Alexis stretched out on the bed and clicked through the ten available channels on the small TV.

"Are you ever going to tell me what this is about?" she asked, stopping on TBS to check out what might be a watchable movie.

"I told you," Swede said. "It's about the research."

"Which tells me nothing."

"Like I said--"

"I know what you said." The movie was some cop flick, full of stupid banter and chase scenes. Alexis muted the sound, tossed the remote aside, and rolled over to face Swede. "You need to tell me more. I wouldn't have even come this far, if you hadn't freaked me out. But I insist on getting a few details. I'm not going any farther with you unless you tell me what's going on."

"I'm trying to protect you." Swede turned from the window. He looked exhausted. "Please. Just trust me."

Alexis considered this. "No."

"No?"

"I need an explanation. You're disrupting my life. I have a master's thesis to work on and classes to attend. And a limited time to finish my studies, so if you're going to insist that I live my life on the run, I have to know why I'm running."

Swede shook his head. "I had hoped to avoid this."

"Clearly, but if you don't explain now, I'm calling a cab or catching a bus back home."

Swede sighed. "Well, I can't really force you to come."

"They call it kidnapping."

Swede grimaced and glanced out the window again. He froze as the flash of headlights illuminated him briefly, then relaxed as they disappeared.

"All right," he said. "Did Daniel ever explain the theory we were testing?"

"I told you. Daniel didn't explain a thing."

"Well, you did know he was a cosmologist."

"Yes, yes. You were both studying the origins of the universe."

Swede grabbed a chair and turned it backward. He straddled it and dropped onto the seat with a grunt, resting his arms on the back, his solid torso settling like a sack of cement. "You've heard of Albert Einstein, of course."

"Gosh, no, Swede. Who's he?"

Swede's mouth turned up on one side, but the half-smile quickly vanished. "You probably know that under Einstein's theory of relativity, the speed of light is constant."

"Yes, I know. I took basic physics, remember? Even thought about majoring in it, but philosophy was a better match for me."

Swede nodded. "That's right. Remind me. Why did you change your mind?"

"Couldn't hack the math. Calculus was my downfall."

Swede nodded. "There's a lot of that."

"Don't change the subject. You were talking about Einstein and the speed of light."

Swede paused, as if gathering his thoughts. "Have you ever heard of João Magueijo?"

"No. What the hell is that?"

"It's a who, not a what." Swede explained that João Magueijo was the name of a Portuguese cosmologist. "He was trying to figure out certain inconsistencies between what we know about the universe and the Big Bang theory."

"Magueijo came up with this notion that maybe Einstein had it wrong. Maybe the speed of light wasn't a constant. To boil it down, if light moved faster than it does now when the Big Bang occurred, it would explain a whole lot of things that hadn't made sense up until then. Like the 'horizon problem.' Are you familiar with that?"

Alexis shook her head.

"Essentially, the background radiation in our universe is too evenly disbursed, too homogeneous. The universe is so huge, this shouldn't be the case. The edges of the universe are 28 billion light years apart, but the universe is only 14 billion years old. If nothing can travel faster than the speed of light, heat radiation simply couldn't have travelled between the two horizons fast enough to even out all the hot and cold spots and create thermal equilibrium throughout the universe." He paused. "I get the feeling I'm losing you."

"I think I get the gist. Just don't start talking in differential equations."

Swede smiled. A real smile this time. "That part doesn't really matter, anyhow. That's just the background. Suffice it to say, it's a controversial theory. He's been heavily criticized for positing it as a better theory than the ones that square with Einstein's views."

"Okay. And all this is dangerous why?"

Swede hunched his shoulders and leaned into the chair. "Magueijo wrote a book called *Faster Than the Speed of Light*. In it, he mentions that the research he was doing might end up being used to create a more powerful weapon than the H-bomb but dismissed this concern in a footnote. Under his theory of VSL--that's variable speed of light--an accelerator used to produce Planck mass particles would create a bomb with half the power of an H-bomb. However . . . ."

Alexis waited. Her life felt worse than a Hitchcock movie.

"Magueijo had a footnote to this in his book. It said that this outcome was based on a certain factor in his equations being positive. But if he was wrong and that factor was negative . . . it would actually create a bomb twice as powerful. At least, in theory."

Alexis drew in a breath. "So you've proved this theory? The one that could lead to . . . oh, my God."

Swede's head drooped. "Not conclusively, but our research led us to believe Magueijo's worst-case scenario could be true." He looked up at Alexis. "And I don't think Daniel's death was an accident."

CHAPTER EIGHT

"Wait a minute, wait." Alexis held up one hand like a crossing guard. "Why would they, whoever they are, want to kill Daniel?"

Swede heaved a sigh and rubbed his forehead. He resumed his watch out the window.

"I'm assuming you meant he was murdered," Alexis said. "Crashing your own car down a steep slope seems like an odd way to commit suicide."

Swede squeezed his eyes shut and his brow furrowed as if conjuring a response took great effort. "We were approached."

"Approached?"

"Three people who claimed to be with the government. They said they'd gotten wind of our research and wanted to know our findings. Daniel and I were suspicious right away, since we'd told no one exactly what we were working on. We asked them where they got their information, but they refused to tell us."

"Could they have checked your records at Stanford and figured it out?"

Swede shook his head. "Stanford makes you fill out a ream of forms before you can use their particle accelerator. They collect lots of information and make sure you're trained . . . ."

"And not a terrorist?"

"Right. I'm sure they've checked our backgrounds. But they don't ask exactly what we're doing." Another vehicle cruised by and a phantom light striped Swede's pale face then faded. "These people had to get the information from another source."

"What about your adviser? You told him, right?"

"Only the bare essentials. That we were testing out Magueijo's VSL theories. We never told him what we found out about the Planck factor. We were afraid." Swede lowered his head into his hands, holding it like a basketball. "I guess we were right to be. I guess we were stupid to keep it a secret."

Alexis tried to wrap her mind around Swede's words, but something wasn't adding up. "How can you be so sure Daniel was killed over this? If they wanted your research, what would they gain from killing him?"

"To get to me. To force me to give it to them."

Alexis shook her head. "I find that hard to believe. Maybe these people *were* with the government. They showed you their IDs, right?"

Swede shrugged. "So what if they did? You think these things can't be forged?"

Alexis peered at Swede. Could there really be something to what he said? Or had all the secrecy around his work with Daniel made him paranoid? Or worse?

Maybe coming with Swede had been a bad idea. She should just play along. At least until she could think of a way to get clear of him.

Swede was shaking his head. "It's all my fault. It was my idea to keep it secret. Daniel agreed, but it was my idea."

"You can't blame yourself," Alexis said, in a voice that sounded dull and unconvincing even to her. *Don't quit your day job for the theatre.* "You did what you thought was right at the time."

Neither spoke for a moment. The cop movie on TV was gearing up for what looked like a big finish. A battalion in SWAT gear huddled outside a brick building, while inside a man and woman did step-turn maneuvers around corners, their arms outstretched with handguns aimed, like Disneyland robots. *It's a Small World--and Very Violent--After All.*

Alexis rubbed her face. Swede's paranoia was exhausting. "So where are we going, anyway?"

"I've been trying to figure that out. Perhaps a big city. Somewhere where we could get lost in the crowd."

Alexis' first thought was Seattle, but was that far enough? Swede stiffened and stared out the window. "Uh oh," he said.

"What is it?" Alexis whispered, although she couldn't imagine why she should do that.

"I'm not sure, but I think . . . ."

φφφ

JESSICA

"Jessica!"

I lurched and my hands jumped from the keyboard. Gasping, I looked up to see Cynthia Dalrymple. One of Fred's friends.

"Cyn. God. You startled me."

"I'm sorry, Jess." Cyn floated over and eased into the chair across from me, tossing a red silk scarf over one shoulder like

Isadora Duncan. Recalling the famous dancer's horrible death by strangulation when her scarf got caught in her car's rear wheel, I caught myself checking behind Cyn for rotating mechanical devices.

Cyn giggled. A bubbly champagne sound. "I forget how wrapped up you get in your writing. What're you working on?"

"Just a story."

Cyn's eyes widened. "Is this the novel? Oh, how cool! How's it coming?"

"Okay, I guess." *It's for shit, but it's going just swell.*

"Oh, I so envy you." Cyn's expression combined rapture and anguish. "I wish I could write. I would so love to be creative like you."

"Not if you want to stay sane," I muttered.

"Pardon?"

"I said, sometimes it overtaxes my brain."

Cyn giggled again. "Overtax *your* brain? Oh, c'mon now. You're a genius." She wrinkled her nose and scrunched her eyelids. "You're such a kidder."

I smiled. "That's me. Jessica the Joker."

"Have you seen Fred?"

It seemed like an odd change of subject. "I've been trying to reach him. I keep getting his voice mail."

"Me, too. Strange." She appeared put out. "Fred was supposed to come to Sherry's party this past weekend?" Cyn had this way of making statements into questions. Drove me nuts. "He didn't show. Not like him. Fred's so social? So I called him and emailed. He hasn't answered." She pouted. "What's up with that?"

"I dunno, Cyn. I don't handle his social calendar." I glanced at my watch, closed out the word processing program, and prepared to leave. Time to move on.

Cyn recoiled. "No need to get bitchy, okay? Just asking . . . ."

I paused before saying anything more. After counting to five (ten would have taken too long), I said, "I didn't mean to snap at you, Cyn. But, really. I don't know what's going on with Fred."

"Of course." She nodded, looking contrite.

"Frankly, I'm a bit worried."

Cyn nodded again. "Yes." She looked up at me. "He has been acting . . . strange?"

I peered at her. "So you've noticed a difference in his behavior, too?"

"He seems depressed, withdrawn. When was the last time you spoke to him?"

I thought back. "I guess it's been two or three weeks."

Cyn's brow furrowed. "That's when I noticed the change in him, too."

"Do you have any clue what it might be?"

Cyn opened and shut her mouth, then spoke. "I can't be sure, but I think it has something to do with you."

"Me?" *What the fuck?*

Cyn stared me in the eyes. "You need to talk to him, Jess. I think you need to get the story straight from him." She tossed her scarf over her shoulder again.

φφφ

I exchanged the bare minimum of chitchat with Cyn, before I made my farewells. I then gathered my things and bundled them into the car. From there, I dialed Fred on my cell phone. Got his voice mail again. Instead of leaving a message, I headed straight for his place, which wasn't far from school. Time to face whatever was going on with the guy.

On the way, I tried to picture what could be wrong. We hadn't argued or had any kind of disagreement. If anything, Fred had bent over backward to help me get inside information that was proving useful in writing the book. He had lots of friends and connections—people who knew about political dissident groups and various anti-government crazies who might want to use Daniel's research for nefarious reasons. The kind of information you can't pick up at the library or even in a Google search.

My car chugged up the hill in the old tree-lined neighborhood, and I eased it up to the curb by Fred's apartment building. From the street, I could see his beat-up green Volvo in the lot. I called his number again. Voice mail. Don't know why I even tried.

I set the handbrake and turned the wheels toward the curb, a habit I picked up while learning to drive in the mountainous sections of Colorado. I got out and approached the white stucco building. The wind blew, and the fan-shaped leaves in the aspen trees trembled and whispered.

I stepped into the foyer and climbed the steps to the third floor, pausing before knocking. *Could Fred be really depressed? Could he have become dangerously unhinged?* I stood there, spinning out all sorts of nightmare scenarios. The product of too much TV (and, of course, reading too many suspense novels). Suddenly, I felt stupid. *Fred wouldn't hurt me. Maybe the guy needs help. I owe him that much after all he's done for me.*

I rapped on the door. No answer. I tried again. Nothing. On impulse, I tried the knob. Unlocked, but that wasn't unusual. Many Boulder residents don't bother locking their doors during the day. I started inside, calling Fred's name, but stopped short when a horrible stench overwhelmed me. Then I saw the wreckage. Someone had fucked the place up good. My jaw dropped involuntarily. I stood there until I spotted bare feet extending out from the kitchen.

I charged in without thinking. Fred was on the floor face up. His skin was waxy, his brown eyes vacant. Head resting in a pool of blood, his smooth brow was marred only by a small hole. Bending over, I felt bile rise in my throat.

CHAPTER NINE

KEVIN

Now that Fred was out of the way, it left the group wide open to do what it would. However, there was still the novelist to deal with. Did Jessica know anything and would it end up in her book? He had to find out. Even if she hadn't written it into the plot, her knowledge was dangerous to the group.

Kevin felt woozy from the drugs. Nonetheless, he knew the group's plans took precedence over even an innocent life.

Sometimes sacrifices had to be made for the greater good.

CHAPTER TEN

JOE

The van crawled up the hill, keeping a safe distance from Jessica's Dodge Dart. Cotter slowed and pulled over, as Jessica parked and got out.

"She's heading to the apartment." Billy spoke in a high-pitched singsong.

Cotter grunted.

Billy shook his head. "Man, she's gonna run now."

"Maybe it's for the best."

Billy stared at him. "But what about . . . ."

"Billy." Cotter struggled to keep his voice low and even. "What did I tell you before?"

Billy's face furrowed in thought. "If she runs, we follow?"

"Right."

"And the others?"

Cotter raised a hand and dropped it. "We'll cross that bridge when we come to it."

"So . . . just keep watching her for now?"

Cotter looked at Billy. "You catch on quick, Sport."

CHAPTER ELEVEN

JESSICA

I felt the room spin at the sight of Fred's corpse. Seeing him dead was like a punch in the gut. From the sight of his pants, it was obvious the stench wasn't just from bodily deterioration. He'd emptied a full bladder and moved his bowels upon death.

The sewage smell was overbearing, so I stepped back outside, gulping the fresher air in the hallway. I shut the door behind me, but the foul odor lingered in my nostrils.

The door across from me opened, and I jumped. I gaped as an old woman came out. She had disconcertingly light blue eyes embedded in wrinkled flesh, and her head was topped with a shock of gray hair. Wrapped in a tattered pink robe, she jangled a set of keys in one palsied hand and held a tissue in the other.

"Are you all right?" Her voice sounded quivery and nasal.

"I . . . I'm okay." I wasn't ready to talk to anyone about Fred yet. Let alone a little old lady in a pink robe in a hallway where I didn't even want to be.

The old woman gave a vague nod, shuffled toward the steps, and descended them, keys jingling all the way.

I stared at the Fred's door and tried not to think of what was behind it. Fred had been acting peculiar, but he hadn't struck me as suicidal and I hadn't seen a weapon. So why would someone kill Fred? What did Cynthia mean when she said it might have something to do with me?

I considered calling the police, but frankly, I didn't want to get involved. I could call in an anonymous tip from a phone booth. Assuming I could still find one. Could they trace the call, if I made it from my cell? Besides, the cops couldn't bring Fred back to life.

I felt dizzy. I backed away from the door, hands raised as if to ward off evil, my thoughts reeling. When did this happen? Who was the last to see him alive?

I followed the old woman down the stairs and caught up with her near a row of mailboxes.

"I'm trying to find your neighbor, but he's not home. When was the last time you saw him? The young man living across from you?"

She blinked slowly, seeming to consider this. "I don't know. Sometime last week, I guess."

"Have you seen any strange people around here?"

She barked a laugh. "This town is full of strange people. And a few of them live here," she said, fumbling to insert the key in one of the mailboxes.

It was grasping for straws, but I had to ask. "Have you noticed a dark van hanging around the parking lot lately?"

She swiveled round to face me. "I don't know. I don't think so."

"Or two men in tan jumpsuits?"

She shook her head as she removed a fistful of mailers and catalogs from the box. I was leaving when I heard her say, "Unless you mean the delivery men."

"Delivery men?"

"Sure. They wore tan jumpsuits. One of them had a clipboard. Figured it was to sign for deliveries. Thought they were bringing me a Snuggie I ordered weeks ago."

"An older man and another one with red hair?"

She smiled. "Yes, one of them was a redhead. I've always thought red hair looks strange on men."

"Thanks," I said, and turned to leave.

"Is something wrong?" she called after me.

"Not a thing. Thanks for your help." I rushed to the car.

φφφ

I could barely keep my hands on the wheel for their shaking. What to do? Call the police? There'd be questions. Another report. Did I want to get involved? Would the killers come after me, if I did? Would the cops suspect me? It happened and not just in mystery novels.

I wanted to go home and think, but the coincidence about the so-called delivery men seemed to suggest it was the last place I should be. If they had killed Fred, why hadn't they killed me?

I pulled over long enough to retrieve my cell phone and place a call to 911.

A woman answered. "Nine-one-one. Please state the nature of your emergency."

"Please send the police to 8111 Mountain Road," I said. "Apartment 3A."

"What's wrong? What is the nature . . . ." I disconnected her in mid-sentence. I'd done right by Fred, without getting further enmeshed in whatever was up.

Putting the phone away, I drove and considered my situation. If the cops didn't think the phone calls and note were threatening, what would they say about my being at a murder scene? Perhaps I'd be better off leaving town for a while.

I tried to calm down, but my foot was heavier than it should have been. I took the turn onto the main road toward my place so fast the car skidded nearly to the curb. At this rate, I was well on my way to killing myself. I glanced in the rear-view mirror just to make sure that Boulder's finest hadn't noticed my recklessness.

Then I saw the dark van, turning off the same side street, heading my way. And everything wasn't fine again.

Could it be the same van? I made an impromptu turn at the next side street and punched the gas to get some distance between me and the main road. I stopped and waited, watching the intersection in my rearview mirror. In a matter of moments, the van appeared and rounded the corner. I pulled a right turn, executing a series of maneuvers highly unlikely to be taken by anyone who wasn't following me. A couple of times I thought they'd gone elsewhere or I'd lost them, but they always reappeared. To their credit, they kept a respectful distance—I'd probably never have noticed them if I hadn't been looking—but I wasn't able to lose them either.

Rather than go home, I headed back to Pearl Street. I needed to come up with a plan. The last thing I wanted was to return home alone with this van on my tail.

I pulled into the first spot I saw near the Pearl Street Mall, a popular pedestrian mall. I got out and looked around. Couldn't see the van, but that didn't mean it wasn't nearby. Glancing around, I strode toward the mall and plunged in among the milling people. I hustled through the throng, despite having no destination. Anxious to get lost in the crowd. (Like Swede had said in my book? Too weird.) I needed time to think.

I'd joined a group of people clustered around a juggler, when I caught a glimpse of a red-haired man walking toward my car. He appeared to be the one I'd seen yesterday morning outside my place. He was dressed in a T-shirt and jeans this time. He pointed toward my car. The older man with him, a tall, middle-aged guy with a graying flattop, also dressed casually, scowled and ignored him, scanning the crowd like the spotlight from a watchtower.

I should've walked away then, but I froze in place, staring at them. The older man's spotlight gaze swept around, until it locked with mine. His expression never changed, but the spark of recognition in his eyes told me I'd been made. He tapped the younger man's arm, nodded and moved into the crowd.

I pushed my way out of the group, drawing several annoyed glances and one exasperated, "Ouch! Watch it!"

"Sorry," I called over my shoulder. Whatever I'd done, I had no time for extensive apologies. All I could think of was to find a place to hide. Quickly.

"Jess!"

I didn't have to look to recognize the voice. Cynthia again. What were the odds I'd see her twice in one day? Not that long, actually, given Boulder's small size. I pretended not to hear and kept going.

"Jess! Hold on!"

I felt a hand on my shoulder and jumped, not sure who I'd see. Cyn stood there, wearing that scarf of hers and looking annoyed.

"I was just a few feet from you. Didn't you hear me?"

This opened the door to a host of potential sarcastic replies. But I said, "I'm sorry. I'm a bit preoccupied."

Cyn eyed me for a moment, then chuckled. "It's that novel, right? Were you gripped with inspiration? Communicating with your muse?"

I wanted to tell her that the only thing inspiring me at the moment was fear and that my muse, if I had one, never deigned to call on me. "Just thinking." I grabbed her arm. "Would you like to have something to eat? My treat."

Cyn's mouth dropped open. "Sure!"

Scanning the crowd for any sign of the Dynamic Duo—and finding little comfort in not seeing them—I steered us toward the nearest restaurant, a trendy pizza place on the corner. Cyn was babbling something and I tried to smile and nod at the right points. I glanced over my shoulder once more before ducking into the restaurant. Caught a glimpse of Red and his friend, Flattop, heading in our direction.

The restaurant was in the usual lull between lunch and dinner, so the place was nearly empty. We were seated right away at a table against the wall. Needless to say, I sat with my back toward it.

"I don't normally eat pizza," Cyn said. "So many carbs."

"Uh huh."

She pointed at me and wrinkled her nose. "But, in your case, I'll make an exception."

"Good."

As I flipped through the menu, the two men wandered in. Given the few others present, it didn't take them long to make me. I ducked behind the menu. What did these guys want?

Cyn kept chattering, but nothing registered. Eventually, she gave me a pointed look.

"You *are* distracted, aren't you?"

"Just a little."

She closed her menu and placed it before her. "Jess, you know what your problem is?"

It was a rhetorical question.

"You're so wrapped up in yourself. People in your life are like props, placed there to serve you."

The two men took a table.

"I'm sorry if I seem that way. I'm going through a difficult time."

She dismissed me with the wave of a hand. "It's always something, Jess." She paused. "God knows, Fred feels that way, too."

The mere mention of Fred's name made my pulse race. I wanted to reach across the table and grab her by her stupid scarf. "What do you know about how Fred feels?" I still spoke of him in the present tense.

Cyn bestowed a pitying gaze. "He's never told you this, and it's really not my place to say anything."

"Just tell me!" I was ready to scream, but added, "Please." To be polite.

She sighed and shook her head. "He cares about you, Jess. Really cares and you . . . well, you've never cared back."

I took a deep breath. "Well, he's never brought it up."

"He's tried, but . . . .you never let him."

"What the hell does that mean?"

"You shut him out. Fred says you're cordial, but never open with him. You hold him at arm's length and never let him get close."

I didn't want to have this discussion. Not now and not with Cyn. I needed to find out who killed Fred and whether that person would be gunning for me next.

"Cyn, I never picked up that kind of vibe from Fred, okay? I know he's a caring guy and all. He's helped me a lot. Maybe if he'd said something to me . . . ." My voice trailed off. Could that be what he'd wanted to meet about? It felt sad, not only because I'd never felt more than friendship toward Fred, but knowing that conversation would be impossible now.

Cyn leaned toward me. "The guy would die for you, Jess." She relaxed back in her chair and studied the menu again, shaking her head. "Love like that doesn't come along every day."

Her words knocked the breath right out of me. *Could Fred have been killed because of me?* I felt sick.

"Excuse me a moment." I pulled myself to my feet and searched for the restrooms.

Cyn glanced up, then did a second take. "Are you okay? You look like you just saw a ghost."

"I'm fine. I just need to . . . to use the bathroom. Be right back."

I stumbled through the maze of tables toward the short hallway with the little hand-carved wooden sign marked "Restrooms," pointing the way with an ornate arrow. I could feel Flattop follow my progress.

I pushed through the ladies' room door and launched myself at the row of sinks. The wave of nausea that had threatened to overcome me began to subside but not completely. Turning one of the taps, I splashed cold water on my face, drenching my shirt collar.

Snatching a couple of paper towels from the holder, I dried myself off. *Okay, now what?*

I had a crazy thought. *What would Alexis do in this situation?*

"Great," I muttered. "I'm asking my own fictional characters for advice."

A cursory scan of the bathroom revealed a small window. Small, but not too small to squeeze through.

Do it now. Cynthia might eventually wonder if I fell in and check up on me. Plus I still needed to shake Tweedle-Dum and Tweedle-Dee.

So I hurried to the window—a pair of tall, rectangular panes latched shut by an aging lock with a long, curved handle. I grabbed the handle and tried to pull it up. It was stuck in place.

I smacked it repeatedly with the heel of my hand. At first, I thought I was getting nothing but a bruised hand. Finally, the latch gave, but only a fraction of an inch.

Next I sat on the floor, leaned back on my forearms (ugh!), placed my foot under the handle and kicked as hard as I could. It moved! I kicked it again and again until the latch gave way.

I pushed the window open with a rusty squeal, threaded one leg after the other through and shimmied out into an alley.

CHAPTER TWELVE

JESSICA

The fact that Alexis and Swede ended up crawling out a bathroom window in order to escape the strange people in the van parked outside their motel room, was an irony not lost on me. After I fled down the alley and made my way back to my car, I went straight home and threw a few essentials into a small bag.

I wanted to get as far out of town as possible. I'd have to dip into my small savings and rely on Visa for the rest, but I had to get away from those men. The police couldn't act as my personal bodyguards, and Fred was dead—beyond anyone's help now. I considered my parents, who lived in the Bay Area, but I didn't want to go running home, possibly bringing trouble with me. And San Francisco didn't seem far enough away.

My sister, on the other hand, was across the country in Washington, D.C. She was a lawyer, so trouble was her business. However, it had been nearly a year since I'd last spoken to Liz. She and our parents weren't on the best of terms. I could only hope she wouldn't perceive my visit to her as an imposition. After mulling my other options (which didn't take long, as there were none), I called Liz, tapping my fingers as her phone rang. "C'mon, c'mon . . . pick up."

The ringing stopped, and I groaned as her recorded voice requested that I leave my name, number, and a brief message.

At the beep, I said, "Liz, it's me, Jess. I'm coming out there on the first plane I can catch. It's . . . it's hard to explain. But call my cell as soon as you get this message."

When I'd closed my bag, I quickly booted up my laptop and checked an online site for same-day flights to D.C. After that was squared away, I'd call Shelley and tell her I had to leave town because of a family emergency. The emergency part was true, anyway.

I stored my laptop and flash drive in their carrying case. Like Alexis, I intended to hold onto these items like grim death. I'd spent way too much time working on my novel to leave it behind.

φφφ

I put my old Dodge into overdrive, rocketing down US 36 to get to the airport in time to inch through the security line.

As I snaked toward the TSA folks, I glanced about looking for the redhead and his taller companion. *Surely, they couldn't have followed me here. Could they?* I checked my watch with OCD frequency, as the line crawled along. By the time I made it through the metal detector, I had 15 minutes to get to the gate.

Hastily re-tying my shoes and cramming cords and accessories back into my laptop case, I snatched up my purse, laptop, and carry-on bag and half-ran, half-stumbled toward the train that would take me to Concourse B. Luckily, I was able to leap aboard just before the doors closed.

I collapsed onto a seat, allowing my baggage to droop to each side, and tried to catch my breath, although the occasional snippets of carnival music they played on the train were hardly relaxing. As we rolled into the concourse, I checked my watch again. Nine minutes—yikes!

I lumbered out the door and onto the escalator, lugging my bag up the moving steps. "C'mon, c'mon." I muttered my new mantra.

Once I reached the top, I hit the ground running. Caught sight of a clock—eight minutes! Could I make it?

Checking the gate numbers, I realized they were going up instead of down. Damn! Wrong direction, stupid.

Pulling a hasty U-turn, I pounded the other way, puffing like an asthmatic steam engine.

As I neared the gate, I veered right, negotiating a series of sharp turns through the rows of seating, toward a bottle-blonde flight attendant, who looked to be closing up her station and making ready to shut the door.

"Wait!" I cried in what must have sounded like intense pain.

The blonde stared at me, wide-eyed and blinking. Upon closer inspection, I could see her face had frequent flyer miles etched into it, but it couldn't have looked more beautiful to me than at that moment.

"Oh, goodness." She smiled. "Almost left withoutcha, dear."

Her Midwestern twang was music to my ears.

φφφ

I strapped myself into seat 15D and tucked my laptop and shoulder bag securely under the seat in front of me. I wanted to try Liz again, but they were already telling us to shut off our cell phones and portable devices. So I tuned out as the flight attendant droned through the usual safety preamble. I shut my eyes and didn't open them until we'd reached an altitude of 35,000 feet.

Feeling more (if not completely) relaxed, I pulled out my laptop with intent to focus on Alexis' story. So where was I? Oh, yes—the van had shown up at the motel and Swede and Alexis snuck out the window. And then? Well, they can't just go to their car, can they? So I reviewed what I'd had them do instead. See if it still worked for me.

φφφ

ALEXIS

Swede peeked out the motel's bathroom window. "Nothing here," he muttered to Alexis and opened it.

After they shimmied through it, Swede scanned the surroundings again.

"First thing we need to do is get some distance between us and this motel," Swede said. Alexis nodded, then followed Swede across the dark, weedy courtyard, toward the woods behind the building. The rain had stopped, but their feet squished on damp, grassy earth. The clammy air held the sharp tang of evergreens.

"Got everything, right?" he asked, hefting his backpack and patting his pocket to check for his wallet.

Alexis went through a quick mental checklist-- purse, laptop, and paper bag luggage. All present and accounted for.

"Yeah," she said. "Let's move out."

Swede nodded, and together they plunged into the woods.

They wandered for a bit through the dank forest, brushing against tree limbs and getting spattered by droplets. The ground was slippery in spots and Alexis felt damp and feathery ferns tickle her calves. She pulled her hood over her head, but the chill penetrated her jacket.

Together, they circled (or, at least, Alexis hoped they were circling) back toward the highway, far enough from the motel so the van's occupants wouldn't notice.

It seemed like they wandered through the woods for a half hour, although it could have been only 10 minutes. Alexis couldn't see her watch in the dark. They tromped in silence until she finally asked, "Are we heading toward the road or what?"

Swede stopped and turned a full circle, as if getting his bearings. "The road should be that way," he said, gesturing left. "We've been walking parallel to it."

"Are you sure about that?" Even in the dim moonlight, Alexis could sense Swede's irritation at the question. But it had to be asked. She didn't feel like spending all night cold, wet, and wandering in circles.

"Why don't we head toward the road," she said, trying to make it sound like a polite suggestion instead of an exasperated demand. "We're probably far enough from the motel by now."

Swede looked like he might argue the point for a moment, then shrugged. "Fine." They started walking again.

Alexis remembered now why she and Swede split up.

"So this research you were talking about," she said, as much to break the uncomfortable silence as anything. "I assume your findings are in a safe place?"

"Yes," Swede said. Something in his voice suggested he had more to say on the subject, but he'd stopped himself. He pointed. "See, there's the road." He picked up his pace and strode toward it.

Alexis ignored his I-told-you-so tone, stumbling blindly over roots and undergrowth trying to keep up. One twisted shrub snagged her foot and nearly sent her sprawling face forward, but she caught herself in time. Swede was getting too far ahead, his silhouette starting to melt into the darkness around them.

"Wait! Hold up!" she called.

Swede turned and came back. "I'm sorry."

Alexis resisted the urge to ask him which part of
this dreadful night he was sorry about.

Together, they resumed their trek toward the road.

"So," Alexis continued. "These so-called
government agents--or whatever they are--want to find
us so they can get their hands on your research
documentation. They don't really need either of us,
if they find it without our help, right?"

"I don't think that'll happen. It's not all in one
place, but I know where most of it is."

"Most of it?"

As they emerged from the woods onto the side of
the road, Alexis glanced toward the motel. She was
surprised to see it still in sight, just barely. It
felt like they'd been hiking for miles.

φφφ

JESSICA

"Something to drink?"

"Huh?" I was pulled from my reverie.

A grinning flight attendant loomed over me. "Would you like
a drink?"

"Just water. Thanks."

She handed me a cup of water and a Lilliputian packet of
peanuts. I sipped and munched, thinking about what Alexis and
Swede would do.

I'd had Swede suggest they call a cab. So how do they get the
number? Through information, stupid. Okay. Whatever. But
should I have them hitchhike? On a desolate road at night? I
reviewed my draft and mulled the options.

φφφ

ALEXIS

"Let's walk a little farther, then I'll call a cab," Swede said, heading away from the motel.

"Did you just say you knew where *most* of the research was?"

Swede nodded.

"What about the rest?"

Swede heaved another sigh. "As a safeguard, Daniel and I decided we should divide the documentation and each of us would hold it in separate places. That way, neither of us knew everything. And we could only work on the project together."

Alexis was too stunned to speak for a moment. "Brilliant."

"At the time, it seemed like a good idea. That way, neither of us could be forced to give all the information to anyone."

And neither of you could sell it to someone else on your own, either, Alexis thought but said nothing.

"Well, this is quite a situation, isn't it?" she said. "Not only are these people chasing me for information I don't have, but they're chasing you for incomplete information." Alexis started laughing. Her laughter increased to almost hysterical proportions. When she finally stopped, she was breathing hard and wiping her eyes.

"Are you all right?" Swede said.

"Sure, sure. This will make a great entry in my memoirs. I'll look back on it and be able to laugh for real--some day."

"Good," Swede said. "Because I need you to be strong for me, Alexis."

"Do tell." Alexis' mouth twisted into a wry grimace.

"We not only need to keep away from those guys, we need to make sure they don't find where Daniel hid his part of the research." He paused. "That's where you come in."

Alexis felt her heart sink. "Because even if I don't know what his research was, they'll figure I might know where the documents are."

"Right."

Alexis glanced over her shoulder at the receding lights of the motel winking in the distance. This night just got better and better.

φφφ

From a roadside diner, they took a cab to the nearest bus station and bought two tickets back to Eugene. Once they arrived, Swede suggested they take a quick look through Alexis' place, saying he might have jumped the gun in overlooking it as Daniel's hiding place. While they were there, Alexis decided to pack a bag before leaving for wherever they were headed. While she tossed randomly selected clothes into a duffle, Swede searched. Then he paced, throwing glances out the window at intervals.

"Do *you* think he would've kept it here?" he asked, out of the blue.

Alexis stopped and thought. "I have no idea. He never told me anything."

"No," Swede said, more to himself than Alexis. "Too dangerous. But where would he keep it?"

"The only thing I can think . . . ."

"Yes?"

"I think his family said something about a safe deposit box." Alexis zipped her bag shut. "When I was in Portland for the memorial service, I seem to recall someone mentioning it."

Swede had stopped pacing and looked intent. "I assume the box was here in Eugene?"

Alexis shook her head. "That I couldn't tell you. I was his fiancé, not his wife. I assumed his family was taking care of . . . all that."

"Could you call them and ask?" Swede looked even more anxious.

Alexis paused. She hadn't spoken to her almost-in-laws since the memorial service. "Gosh, I don't know . . . ."

"Please!" Swede blurted. "There's a lot at stake here. A threat to national security even."

"You're right, of course." Alexis might have an awkward phone call in store, but national security trumped her discomfort.

φφφ

JESSICA

I saved the file and shut down my laptop as the plane descended into Dallas, where I would make my connecting flight to D.C. I'd already scoped out the passengers during a trip to the restroom. No redheads or buzz cuts in evidence. I shook my head, feeling slightly ridiculous.

I was looking forward to seeing Liz, but I wondered what I'd tell her. She'd never believe the truth. I could scarcely believe it myself.

CHAPTER THIRTEEN

JOE

Cotter and Billy surveyed the living room of Jessica's empty condo. "Looks like she blew outta here, huh?" Billy said. "I think we freaked her out."

"Your sheer brilliance is surpassed only by your ability to state the completely obvious," Cotter observed.

Billy frowned. "Huh?"

"Exactly."

The freckled redhead muttered, shook his head. "So we blew it."

Cotter's eyes flashed. "Did we? Or did we do her a favor?"

Billy nodded. "Yeah. I see what you mean."

Cotter retrieved his cell phone and made a call. "She's gone," he said into the phone. A moment passed, then he added, "Is that so?" Cotter nodded and said, "Okay, thanks." He ended the call.

"Here's the latest. She's flown the coop. Literally."

He sighed and shrugged. "Like I said, maybe it's for the best."

"But the others—"

"I know." Cotter cut him off. "We still have a job to do."

"Couldn't we just . . . talk to her?"

Cotter looked at him. "That would be nice, but I'm following orders here."

"So what's next?"

Cotter pulled out his cell phone and punched in a number. As the phone at the other end rang, he said, "We need to hop the next plane to D.C."

CHAPTER FOURTEEN

JESSICA

I waited, laptop case leaning against my bag, and scanned the throng of traffic moving through National Airport (I refuse to add Reagan to the name). I'd reached my sister while waiting for my connecting flight in Dallas. Liz seemed happy to hear from me, even eager to see me. Truly odd. I'd expected at least a bit of resistance, if not indignation, given the last-minute nature of my appearance.

I spotted Liz's cherry red Porsche, not exactly the least conspicuous of cars, as it cruised around the curve toward the pickup area. I waved and grabbed my bags as she eased up to the curb.

She slid out, tapped around the car in high heels, and embraced me in a cloud of expensive, spicy fragrance. "It's so good to see you."

"It's good to see you, too," I said. "I really appreciate this."

Liz studied my face, then smiled. She had obviously come from work, despite the late hour. She wore a gray linen suit, the skirt's accordion wrinkles suggesting time spent at her desk at the Justice Department. She tucked a wayward strand of blonde hair behind her ear.

"Let me help you with your bags," she said. "You must be starving. I know just the place to eat . . . ."

After subsisting for the past few hours on Starbucks coffee, a prepackaged sandwich grabbed on the run in Dallas, plus a thimbleful of airplane peanuts, I couldn't have agreed more. As we placed my bags in the trunk, I took one last glance around the crowd and saw nothing of concern.

Everything's fine. You're safe here.

If only I could believe that.

φφφ

It was nearly midnight when we arrived at a restaurant on Capitol Hill, a historic-looking place, all done up in mahogany and brass. We slid into a velvet-cushioned booth and scanned the menu.

"I didn't know anything was open this late in D.C.," I said. "I thought they rolled up the streets around eight."

Liz ignored my little slam at D.C.'s nightlife and kept reading. She still hadn't asked me why I was here.

"Everything looks good," I said.

"Everything *is* good." Her tone turned surprisingly sharp. Setting the menu aside, she added, "The food that is." She peered at me across the table. "Jess, what's going on?"

Here it was. I'd been wrestling with how much to tell Liz and how much to leave out. Given Liz's high-level attorney job, did I really want to tell her about Fred's murder? Or the fact that I'd found him dead and told no one? I had absolutely no idea what obligations, if any, she'd have if I told her.

I launched into the little speech I'd prepared, only to be interrupted by our waiter. After we'd placed our orders, I told her everything—everything except the part about Fred. Instead I said I'd tried to talk to him but couldn't, which, strictly speaking, was true.

Liz mostly listened, her expression patient, her eyes serious, but with a hint of sympathy in them. Now and then, she'd ask for clarification of some point or my thoughts on why this was happening. I could picture her wearing that same face and asking similar questions while meeting with someone from a client agency.

By the time I'd finished my story, our food had arrived and I tucked into my cheeseburger with gusto. Its smoky flavor was intoxicating. Liz poked about at her salad.

"I know you must think I'm crazy," I said, between mouthfuls. "But I just felt like I had to leave. Go somewhere that felt safe, you know?"

"Sure." Liz sounded uncertain, distracted for a moment. She stopped torturing her salad. "You did the right thing."

She returned to her food, then added, "And, no, I don't think you're crazy. Although it does sound rather strange."

You have no idea, I thought.

After we ate, we drove directly to Liz's Capitol Hill condo. Parking was a bitch. Liz just managed to squeeze the Porsche into a spot four blocks away. She couldn't abide the thought of paying for a space. After securing a bar lock on the steering wheel, she locked the car and set the alarm.

"Does it worry you to park such a nice car on the street?"

Liz shrugged. "If they want to steal it, they will. That's what insurance is for."

As we trooped the four blocks past genteel brick row houses, I thought, *Who'd want to live in this berg?* Liz saw it differently, of course. She liked being a Washingtonian. She actually thought it was exciting to have a senator living in her neighborhood. Whoopee.

Liz had a first-floor unit in a rowhouse of whitewashed brick—a tiny, but no doubt expensive, piece of real estate. The one small bedroom barely elevated it above the level of an efficiency. She placed her purse and keys on a small table near the door.

"Let me take the futon," she said. "You can have the bed." She unfolded the futon so it could serve its function as a cot.

"No, I'll take the futon. I don't want to put you out. You've done enough for me already."

"Are you sure?"

I nudged her aside. "I'll be fine, Liz. I'm so tired, I could sleep on the floor."

Liz hesitated, then relented. "Well, okay, if you insist." She smiled. "I'll let you get some rest, then. Got an early morning myself tomorrow. There's cereal in the cupboard, eggs in the fridge, bagels in the freezer . . . ." Her voice trailed off and it hit me how drained she looked. "Just help yourself to anything you like."

"Thanks, sis. Now get some sleep."

"You, too. We can talk more about this tomorrow, if you like."

"I appreciate that. G'night."

"Night."

I watched her shuffle off to bed. I was exhausted, but wired. Probably all that Starbucks coffee on top of eating late. By the time I changed into my PJs, brushed my teeth, and stretched out on the futon, I hoped I'd be sleepy. But the events of the last couple of days kept reeling through my mind like a never-ending movie montage.

Finally, after half an hour of lying still with my eyes shut, I gave up and turned on the TV, keeping the sound low. I flipped through the channels halfheartedly, stopping abruptly on CNN when I saw the words "Murder in Boulder" emblazoned across the bottom of the screen.

If I wasn't wide awake before, I was now. I sat up and tapped the volume up.

". . . victim of the execution-style killing has been identified as Fred Berwin, a graduate student at the University of Colorado."

A picture of Fred flashed to the anchor's right.

"Not since Jon Benet Ramsey has a murder so shaken people in this otherwise quiet university town . . . ."

The anchorman droned on about the police revealing few details concerning the murder and their theories. I wondered when the picture was taken. Fred looked different somehow. Maybe happier. Before I could decide, the picture was gone.

Only to be replaced with mine.

"Police are seeking another university student for questioning. Jessica Evans, who was last seen leaving Berwin's apartment, is considered a person of interest. Police refuse to divulge Evans' relationship to the victim, but other sources confirm they knew each other . . . ."

I sank back onto the mattress. So much for feeling safe.

CHAPTER FIFTEEN

KEVIN

So Jessica had taken flight. And the news was painting her as a likely suspect in Fred's murder. This was working out even better than he'd expected.

Kevin had plans for Jessica Evans. She might run, but she couldn't hide.

CHAPTER SIXTEEN

JESSICA

By the time I awoke later that morning, Liz had already gone to work. I wondered if she'd heard about the murder. Did Liz watch CNN? If it was on CNN, it was probably in *The Washington Post*, too.

Even though I hadn't done anything, I worried that Liz could be accused of harboring a fugitive.

I got Liz's Mr. Coffee brewing and searched the kitchen for breakfast choices, rejecting Liz's healthy cereal, which looked more like bird food than breakfast. As I waited for my bagel to toast, I agonized over the implications of hiding out in her place. Holing up here could put Liz's bar license at risk.

But where would I go? I'd already left the state. Should I turn myself in to the D.C. or Boulder police? My previous dealings with the Boulder cops were less than satisfying. And I didn't treasure the thought of being held on suspicion in a D.C. jail.

The toaster oven dinged, snapping me to attention. As I went through the motions of buttering the bagel and eating it, I thought again about the van, the strange phone calls, and the note. I had nothing to feel guilty about. I'd done nothing wrong.

But the thought of dealing with the police was not a pleasant prospect. I didn't know why Fred was dead. I couldn't be sure that Red and Flattop were the ones who killed him.

Maybe I should just pretend I never saw the news.

For the moment, I wanted—needed, really—to focus on something else. So I poured myself some coffee and did what I often do to distract myself. I set my laptop up and reviewed my draft, starting at the point where Alexis and Swede had reached Portland and were trying to access Daniel's safe deposit box.

φφφ

ALEXIS

"Dude, I nearly forgot about that box," Lena said.

Alexis wasn't sure if Daniel's elder sister was talking to her or to Swede when she said this. They were sitting in the sunny kitchen of the old house in southeast Portland that Lena shared with three other people.

"You think we could have a look at it?" Alexis asked. Her eyes were drawn to Lena's arms, both covered with elaborate tattoos fully exposed by the tight, black spaghetti-strap top she wore. One arm was a study in bright, happy images. The other featured flames and grotesque, demonic faces. Heaven and hell, she thought.

Lena shrugged. "Can't see why not." She took one last drag on her cigarette and snubbed it out in a chipped, ash-laden green saucer. "The bank's on my way to work. We can stop by. I've got time."

Alexis noticed Lena hadn't even checked her watch before saying this, as if she always had time.

At a Washington Mutual Bank on Woodstock Boulevard, Lena spoke with a bank manager and arranged to unlock the safe deposit box. While Lena and the bank manager retrieved the box, Alexis and

Swede waited at a table in a private room, where they could all view the box's contents. Lena entered holding a small box with a latched top. She joined the others at the table and opened it. Inside, there was an envelope.

It was marked: "For Alexis (private)."

"Obviously, this was meant for just me to read," Alexis said, sounding apologetic, although she couldn't think what she had to apologize for.

Lena gave Swede's upper arm a playful jab with her fist--hard enough for Swede to flinch. "Let's give the girl some room." She placed a firm hand on Swede's back and led him out. He glanced back at Alexis, obviously curious.

When they had left, Alexis tore open the envelope. Inside, was a letter:

Dear Alexis,

If you're reading this, it means the worst has happened. I'm probably dead, possibly in the hospital in a coma. I know it upset you that I could never talk about my work. But if something's happened to me because of foul play, you may be in danger, too. In any case, my research must get into the right hands.

I kept my papers in this box for a long time, but recently decided it was too obvious a place. So I leave this letter instead and hope that it reaches you and only you (I think Lena will respect my wishes in this regard).

You may recall a conversation we had shortly after I proposed . . . .

φφφ

Alexis thought back. She did recall Daniel saying that if anything happened to him, she should contact her younger sister, Katie, in New York about his research. She'd been confused, even angered, by this.

"Why are you sharing information about your research with my sister but not me?" she demanded.

"Please understand," Daniel had said. "I'm doing this to protect you."

Alexis had argued the point but had gotten nowhere. Eventually, she'd given up and simply said she understood, even though she didn't. She'd been so pissed off, she'd even considered breaking their engagement. However, she couldn't deny that she still loved Daniel, so she'd let the matter go. By the next morning, she'd cooled off and things looked much brighter. And instead of staying angry, she pushed the whole incident out of her mind.

Alexis stared at the letter, realizing Daniel must have known she might forget to follow through on his instructions. She resumed reading.

You may recall a conversation we had shortly after I proposed. First, I want to apologize for making you feel so marginal to my career. Second, I need you to do as I asked and reach out to your sister. It's essential for getting my work into the right hands.

I can only hope you understand why I've done this. The highly competitive world in which I work has made this necessary.

I wish I could say or do more, but I'll just close with this advice: be careful.

Love,

Daniel

PS: Don't tell <u>anyone</u> else what you're doing.

CHAPTER SEVENTEEN

Reading that letter may have been the hardest thing
Alexis had been made to endure so far. Daniel's words
coming to her from beyond the grave. That was creepy,
as if his ghost were whispering in her ear. To keep
from crying, she bit her lip so hard, she almost drew
blood.

After taking a few moments to compose herself,
Alexis thought about the implications of Daniel's
closing words. *Don't tell <u>anyone</u> else what you're
doing.* By anyone, could he have meant Swede? But
Swede was his partner. He couldn't have meant Swede,
too--or could he?

Alexis replaced the note in the envelope, folded
it, and stuck it in the pocket of her jeans. She
picked up the box and got up to leave but stopped
short. "What do I tell them?"

She could just tell them it was a private letter,
which was true. But Swede would no doubt wonder why
Daniel took the trouble to put it in a safe deposit
box.

No, she'd have to lie. Tell them something that would raise no questions, or at least fewer questions.

Clutching the box, she walked to the door and pulled it open to find Swede and Lena waiting in the hall.

"So?" Lena said. "I'm dying of curiosity here."

Swede just stared at Alexis.

Alexis cleared her throat. "The letter was about life insurance he'd taken out. He never told me, and he wanted to make sure I was paid, if something happened to him." She decided to stop there.

"You're kidding. Why would he go to the trouble of putting that in a safe deposit box?" Lena pursed her lips and blew out a dismissive sputtering noise. Alexis just shrugged in response.

Swede's gaze remained pinned to Alexis' face. He looked disappointed, plus . . . an emotion she couldn't quite nail down.

"Nothing more?" he said, his voice disbelieving.

"It didn't have what we were looking for."

That part was true, anyway.

φφφ

JESSICA

I stopped work and checked the clock. Just after noon. By now, Liz had probably read the headlines or heard the news from someone else. She could be at lunch when it scrolled across the bottom of a TV set at a local take-out deli or even a casual restaurant. Of course, Liz was so Type A, she probably ate a brown-bag lunch at her desk. As a busy Justice Department attorney, would she really pick up on an item in the many news headlines about a murder in Boulder? Perhaps she would because of what I'd told her and my hasty departure to visit her.

My cell phone rang. *Probably Liz wanting an explanation.* But the ID said "Private Caller." My heart sank. *Not again.* I considered ignoring it but decided they'd probably keep ringing if I did.

"Yes," I answered, anyway.

"Jessica." That androgynous voice again. So familiar, but . . . not recognizable.

"What do you want?"

"We need to talk."

"So talk."

"Not on the phone. I need to meet you."

I shook my head, as if the caller could see me. "That's not possible."

"I'm not going to hurt you. I'm trying to help."

"Help how? Besides, I'm . . . ." I didn't continue. I didn't want to talk about where I'd gone.

"I know. You're in D.C. So am I."

I opened my mouth, but nothing came out at first. "You followed me?"

"It's important that we talk. But we have to meet," the caller said.

"Why?"

"Because I can't talk on the phone. Too risky. And the men in the van have followed you here, too."

"What?!" *Jesus. Who are those guys?* "Did those men . . . do that to . . . ."

"Your friend?"

"Yes, my friend," I said.

"I wouldn't trust them."

I suppressed the urge to scream. "You still haven't explained . . . ."

"It will all be explained, Jessica." A long pause, then, "But not over the phone."

"I don't know." I ran through the possibilities. If we met at a park or restaurant, what's the worst that could happen? But D.C. wasn't Boulder. If I were abducted in broad daylight, would anyone notice or care? My imagination was working overtime again.

"Jessica," the voice implored. "Think of your sister."

My blood froze. "What about her?"

"You don't want her to get hurt, do you?"

It felt as if my lungs had collapsed.

"Think about it," the voice said. "I'll call you back in ten minutes."

The line went dead.

CHAPTER EIGHTEEN

JESSICA

It felt like an eon had passed before I closed the phone and put
it down. The last thing I wanted was for Liz to get involved in
this. She had nothing to do with it—whatever *it* was.

The threat was clearly intended to intimidate me. It worked. I
planned our meeting. Assuming the caller was a man, I should
pick a public place with lots of people around. Navy Memorial.
I'd met Liz there for lunch a couple of times. There was a Metro
stop close by an amphitheater of steps arranged around a
fountain where people gathered for lunch.

The phone rang and I jumped. That hadn't been ten minutes.
The caller ID showed that it was Liz. My finger wavered over
the button, until the fourth ring when I pushed it.

"Hey, you," Liz said, sounding carefree, almost giddy. Not
like someone who'd discovered her sister was sought for
questioning in a murder. "I'm just heading out to lunch. Want to
join me?"

"I'm . . . feeling a bit tired, actually. And I'm making progress
on my book." I winced after saying that. Why did I mention the
book? Now she's going to think the book's more important
than she is. "How about tomorrow?"

"Sure." Liz seemed unfazed. "I'm forgetting you just flew in last night. The time zone adjustment and all."

"Yeah," I said, feeling uncertain about the difference two hours would make to a person's internal clock.

Liz jabbered on about where we could go for dinner and places we could see. I kept glancing at the clock. It was coming up on ten minutes.

"Well," Liz said, probably sensing my distraction. "Don't work too hard. I'll see you tonight."

"Right."

I snapped the phone shut, clutching it like a talisman, waiting for the promised callback. Ten minutes arrived. No call. Twelve minutes. Nothing. *What kind of threatening anonymous caller are you, anyway?*

At thirteen minutes, I set the phone aside and tried to concentrate on reviewing my story again. Not easy, especially since I'd written that Alexis would give Swede the slip and reserve a last-minute flight to New York to see her sister. She'd book the flight online, of course—the resemblance to my life was getting eerie.

Despite my anxiety, I realized I should probably stop for lunch. Getting stressed out takes lots of energy, making me tend to crave food. I was considering my lunch options, when the phone rang. Private caller.

I answered by saying, "That was a long ten minutes."

"Jessica, have you thought about what I said?"

"Yes. I'll meet you at the Navy Memorial."

"I was thinking of . . . something more private."

"No way. You've been calling the shots so far. I get to pick the meeting place."

I expected more of a protest, but the caller just said, "All right. Just be careful."

CHAPTER NINETEEN

JOE

Cotter and Billy had rented a car—not quite as suitable for their needs as a van, but the budget on this job was getting tighter by the moment. They chose a bland gray midsized vehicle—not anything too cop-like, but not too showy either.

As Cotter eased the car into a tight parking spot down the street from Liz's place, he wondered if a compact car would have been a wiser choice.

But he managed to back into the spot with little fuss, not even bumping the curb. With a satisfied sigh, Cotter said, "Now we wait."

Billy nodded amiably. Both men stared down the street toward Liz's building.

They were prepared for a long haul. They'd bought sandwiches for lunch and plenty of bottled water.

Hours ticked by. By quarter past noon, Cotter decided it was time for lunch. He dug into a sandwich and Billy followed suit.

Between bites, Cotter pulled out his cell phone and dialed a number.

At the other end, his client said, "Yes?"

"Just to let you know, no movement. In or out."

"Okay, thanks."

Cotter closed his phone and finished his sandwich in three bites.

"Surveillance sucks," Billy grumbled.

"Tell me about it."

"She's bound to stay in there all day. What with the news and all."

Cotter nodded. "Probably. Question is, who'll try to come to her?"

Billy grunted assent. Cotter felt like his eyes might cross if he had to stare at the building much longer. Both men jolted when Jessica emerged and scurried down the front steps. Cotter could tell it was her, although she wore a pair of dark glasses and a floppy hat. She nibbled on a snack as she walked, head bowed, but swiveling now and then, as if to check her surroundings.

Cotter weighed the possibilities. She could be taking the subway or cab. Or she could be walking. The safest alternative for a fugitive seemed to be a cab.

She had passed them going down the opposite side of the street, when he started the car.

"Won't she notice us?" Billy said.

"Not if we take it slow. And careful."

"I thought that's what we were doing before."

Cotter gave him a hard look. "This time, we'll do it better."

CHAPTER TWENTY

JESSICA

So much for lunch. I snatched a granola bar from Liz's stash, headed out the door, and took a right toward the main road. I thought about the subway, but worried that the Metro security people might recognize me, despite my feeble attempts to disguise myself. Assuming I could remember where the nearest Metro stop was.

I felt ridiculous in the hat that I'd found in Liz's closet, but it had a nice, wide brim that flopped over my face just enough to hide my features. I couldn't help feeling it was just a touch too sophisticated for my jeans and T-shirt. At least it was a silk T-shirt. Still the hat seemed to cry out to be matched with something more like a little black dress or a long gown like Holly Golightly wore in *Breakfast at Tiffany's*. Hopefully, it wouldn't have the opposite effect of making me even more conspicuous.

I was idly considering the possibility of taking up smoking through a long-handled cigarette holder and living the Bohemian life—just me and a cat holding parties every night in a New York apartment—when I reached the corner and noticed a couple of cabs roll by. Hmm. Should I take a cab or walk? The walk was several blocks. Now, in Boulder, several blocks is nothing. In D.C., even one block can seem close to a mile. It depends on which block you're talking about. On the stretch of Constitution Avenue I was headed for, a block could stretch out for some distance.

"Oh, hell." I waved down the next cab I spotted. He pulled up to the curb, with an abrupt squeak of tires.

As I climbed in and pulled the door shut, I said to the Plexiglas partition behind the driver, "Could you take me to the Navy Memorial on Constitution, pl—"

The cab took off with a squeal of tires—so fast I was thrown back against the seat.

The cabbie's radio was tuned to NPR. I pulled the hat's brim lower over my face. If this guy listened to NPR, he might follow the news in other media. He might have seen my picture in the papers, on the Web, or on TV. It was hard for me to fathom. *I'm just a student, not a killer,* I wanted to snivel.

Fortunately, the cab driver was so busy trying to wreck his car, barreling through yellow lights turning red as we hit the intersection and taking the cab through slalom turns around slower-moving vehicles (which is to say, everyone else), I doubt my face even registered on his radar. For my own part, I simply clung with grim determination to the seat back and sent up a prayer or two. I've never considered myself particularly religious, but there are no atheists in D.C. cabs.

I arrived at my destination in one piece. I was so grateful, I threw in a couple of extra bucks toward the tip. The driver smiled, his teeth gleaming from a mahogany face. His right front tooth was rimmed with gold. "Have a good day, miss," he said, with an accent that sounded British, and he barreled back into the traffic.

I stood by the curb and looked around. The caller said he'd know me. Before we'd hung up, I'd asked him (assuming it was a "him") how he knew me, but he'd never answered the question.

I walked toward people congregated on the amphitheater steps surrounding the Navy Memorial. Many were seated and enjoying a late lunch or just talking, legs stretched out, and soaking up the sun.

I moved toward the crowd, scanning it with each step. I wondered if he'd already seen me. I felt eyes on my back and whirled around to see a cop car, creeping by.

I turned away and hustled into the throng, which was growing dense with people coming out of the Metro.

Pulling the hat's brim down and peering out from beneath it, I looked at the street. The cop car wasn't there. I exhaled, releasing the tension that had hiked my shoulders halfway to my ears.

I continued to thread my way through the ever-increasing crowd. A small band with keyboard, guitars, and drums was setting up in a roped-off area below. The guitarist was tuning, and another man was testing mics. My nerves had made my mouth so dry, I thought my tongue might stick to the roof of my mouth. In the distance, I saw a deli. Desperate for water, I headed toward the deli, diagonally up the steps, sidestepping audience members. The crowd thinned out in the plaza at the top.

I glanced back. The woman behind me stopped short when I looked at her. I held my gaze a moment too long for her comfort, apparently. She turned away and hurried off.

Surveying the area one last time, before entering the deli, I shook my head. *What am I doing?*

I walked inside and ordered a large bottled water. Moments later, clutching the bottle, I emerged into the sunlit plaza.

The band was warming up now. I figured I'd stand at the edge of the crowd until my "date" appeared.

I felt a light touch on my elbow and heard the voice. "Jessica?"

I caught my breath and turned. The man was short with sandy, disheveled hair and an incipient beard that would have looked grungy cool if his expression weren't so distraught. He looked oddly familiar.

"You're the one who called me?" I said.

He nodded. "Let's take a seat," he said, in the husky voice I recognized from the calls.

We worked our way through the crowd on the steps and sat among the spectators.

"So what's going on?" I asked, after sipping my water.

He frowned. "You need to keep away from the two men who are following you."

"I may be slow, but I've figured that much out." I took another drink, but my mouth still felt gluey. "First things first, though. Who are you?" I said, enunciating with care, since my dry lips felt stuck to my teeth.

"I guess you don't remember. Fred introduced us once. On campus?"

"Right!" I remembered then where I'd seen him. We'd been walking across campus and this man—clean-shaven at the time—had approached. Fred had seemed uncomfortable but still introduced him. I tried to think of the name. Something unusual.

"Selby," he said, as if reading my mind. "Selby Harris."

"Yes! I remember now." I took another swig of water and waited for Selby to go on. When he didn't, I said, "So, Selby, what the hell is going on? Did those men kill Fred?"

"To be honest, I don't know if they did. I don't even know who they are, but if I were you, I wouldn't trust them."

I started to agree, then stopped myself. "Hold on. If you don't know anything about them, how come you don't trust them?"

"How come you don't?"

Because they followed me from Fred's place and they've been spying on me, I wanted to say. Instead, I held my tongue. I wanted to hear his thoughts, unadulterated by my own opinions.

"That's not an answer," I finally said. "In fact, you still haven't told me anything. Like, why all the secrecy? Why couldn't we talk on the phone? And what's this all about, anyway?"

Selby's glance darted around. The band launched into its first number. Classic rock, sounding like the Rolling Stones or maybe the Kinks. He said something I could barely hear for the music.

"What?" I yelled.

"I said, it's about your book."

"About my book?" I scowled and leaned toward him, so he could hear me. "Why would someone kill Fred because of my book?"

"Because of the research he did for you. He was putting himself in danger."

"What do you mean?" I said, after nearly doing a spit-take.

"He was infiltrating extremist groups. Getting inside information."

Suddenly, my mouth turned desert dry. I swigged water, but gulping it down took effort.

"Please tell me you're kidding."

Selby shook his head, his eyes aglow with—what? Fear? Madness?

"I know what he was up to, Jessica. I know because I was in one of those groups."

"So . . . I don't understand. I'm just writing fiction, not spying."

Selby's stare bore holes through me. "You have to understand how these people think. Any outsider could be perceived as threatening."

"So how did he get involved if they didn't trust him?"

Selby stared at his feet. "It was my fault. I was his source. I . . . I realized I was in too deep with the wrong people." He matched my gaze again, with a hint of defiance. "They were supposed to be protecting our freedom. Keeping our government honest. But they turned out to be selfish bastards. And the things they talked about doing . . . ." He shook his head, looking away. "They were using *my* knowledge, but I didn't want anything to do with them after a while."

"And if you stopped associating with them?" I asked, knowing what the answer would be.

He snorted. "It's like leaving the Mafia. You don't. Not without dangerous consequences."

I couldn't believe what I was hearing. "Let's get back to those guys in the van. You said you don't trust them. Why?"

"They could be hired killers. Or—"

I waited for the rest of his answer. One look at Selby and I realized I wouldn't be getting it anytime soon.

He was doubled over, gasping for breath.

I placed my hand on his shoulder and moved closer, so I could hear him over the music. "What's wrong?"

He lifted his head. "My . . . neck . . . ."

I examined his neck. A tiny hole was visible on the back. From a poisoned pin or dart maybe? Selby moaned and seemed barely able to hold his head up.

"Go!" he croaked.

I craned my neck. The family seated behind us seemed oblivious to Selby and me. I stood, and my gaze swept the crowd for anyone running or looking suspicious. I kept my hand on Selby. "What about you? You need help."

"Just go," he said. "They've probably seen you . . . so go . . . now . . . ."

I squatted down. "If they got to you, why didn't they hurt me? You said they could be hired killers or—who?"

Selby licked his lips and struggled to speak. "Ho . . . ."

His voice trailed off and he doubled over completely. My chest tightened and my heart thumped so hard, I could've sworn people heard it as a backbeat to the song being played. I wanted to scream, but I couldn't get my voice to work. *This is like a bad dream!* Even if I could scream, the last thing I needed was to call attention to myself. I could feel panic rising from my pelvis to my throat. People were on their feet now, clapping along to the music, heedless to the man dying on the steps. It seemed like an ideal time to leave.

CHAPTER TWENTY-ONE

JESSICA

I turned to my neighbor with unfeigned panic. "This man's having a heart attack!" Then I pushed through the crowd as fast as I could, hoping that no one had noticed me talking with Selby, who was now doubled over and possibly dying at their feet.

As I broke free of the masses, I heard a woman scream and a babble of voices. I struggled to maintain my composure and ignore the hysteria behind me.

I strode down the sidewalk, scanning for cabs. And cops. And men in trench coats. Men in black with sunglasses. Trench coats and sunglasses? Please. The killers probably wore jeans and T-shirts. The thought raised goose bumps. They could be anyone. Male, female. Anyone at all.

Standing at that curb, I felt as exposed as a target in an arcade game.

I spotted an available cab. My arm shot up, waving as if to a rescue ship from a desert island.

Once settled into the cab, I thought about my conversation with Selby. He had been with a group of political dissidents. Extremists was his term. He had provided Fred an "in" with this group. Fred found out too much—about what? Selby said the group was talking about doing things that prompted him to leave, at risk to his own life. That suggested they were up to something extraordinarily bad.

And he'd emphasized that they were using *his* knowledge. So what did all this have to do with my book? Fred never told me what Selby studied, but if it was physics, it suggested some ugly possibilities.

Fred might have been doing research on how political extremists would react if the scientific premise of my novel— the ability to create a weapon twice as powerful as an atom bomb—proved to be possible.

Good God.

By trying to extract information on terrorist angles, had Fred sent up a red flag? Had he, in fact, been killed trying to help me get information for my book? Worse still, was it because the group was planning something big—something on the scale of 9/11 or worse—that would involve the *kind* of weapon I was writing about? Was that the thing that provoked Selby Harris to flee the group?

I lay back against the bench seat and took deep, even breaths and tried to empty my mind of all thoughts. Later. I'll figure it out later.

At my request, the cab stopped near a coffee shop I'd seen on the way to Liz's the previous night. As I sat, counting out the fare and figuring the tip, I saw the shop's door open. The two men from the van emerged. I froze and stared at the tall man I called Flattop and his younger red-haired assistant, remembering Selby's warning about them.

Shit! Did these guys really follow me halfway across the country to kill me, too?

Then Liz emerged and called the taller man back to have a few words with him. I thought my heart had stopped.

The cabbie cleared his throat. "Um, we're here, miss."

"No." The word leapt from my mouth, as reflexively as a muscle twitch. "Actually, I've changed my mind. Could you take me somewhere else?" I said, my voice quavering despite myself.

φφφ

I had the driver make a quick detour to Liz's place and had him wait while I stuffed the few belongings I'd removed back into my bag and grabbed my laptop. I left Liz's hat where I'd found it. Frankly, I wanted to avoid thinking about Liz. I didn't know what was going on, and maybe I wasn't giving her a fair shake by sneaking out this way. I had no idea why she'd be talking to those men or vice versa. I was beginning to wonder if I should check myself into the psych ward at the nearest hospital, in anticipation of the nervous breakdown I was no doubt going to have soon.

Anyplace, I thought. Dupont Circle came to mind, because Liz and I had gone to dinner at a restaurant there. There were a lot of restaurants lining that section of Connecticut Avenue. Surely, there'd be a hotel around somewhere.

After I hopped back into the cab, I asked, "Can you recommend a cheap hotel in Dupont Circle?"

The driver smirked. "Cheap hotel? I don't think so."

"Can you recommend one anywhere?"

The driver's brow furrowed. "Well . . . not one good enough for a young lady like you."

I threw up my hands. "It doesn't have to be dirt cheap. Are you sure you can't think of a decent hotel that's not too expensive?"

The cabbie appeared to relent. "Possibly. Dupont Circle, you said?"

"Anyplace halfway decent."

He nodded. "The Dupont Plaza. An old hotel. Remodeled. Not cheap but not as expensive as the others."

φφφ

When I got to The Dupont Plaza, I checked in and went straight up to my room—making sure to turn the deadbolt and attach the chain. Not that it wouldn't give to a swift kick. Sighing, I placed my bag down and set my laptop up on the table.

I stood and gazed out the eighth floor window. People milled about in the street far below, so distant, so oblivious to me and my problems. Ordinary people, living ordinary lives. Feeling bored, unhappy, stuck in lousy jobs or bland marriages. How I envied them.

Somewhere out there was a killer. Or killers.

Selby, the man I'd just met, was once with an extremist group. He was killed, perhaps for leaving the group, knowing what they had planned, talking to Fred or talking to me. But by whom?

Selby said the men in the van might be assassins. But my sister wouldn't get involved with anyone like that. Maybe they told her they were someone else. Possible. But still, Liz is no fool. She'd ask for identification, if they told her they were cops or something. Of course, you can get fake IDs.

I walked to the side table and picked up the remote. I turned the TV on to CNN to see if there was an update about Fred or me. I figured Liz had to know by now, and it hurt to think that I hadn't talked to her about it.

The CNN anchor was doing a report on heightened airport security and the threat of terrorist attacks. My ears perked up at these words, but most of the report was delivered in generalities. More of the usual hype. Orange alerts and intelligence reports seemed to have become part of the background noise of modern life.

I reviewed the bizarre revelations and events of the last few days and couldn't help thinking how much my life was imitating my own art.

φφφ

ALEXIS

Alexis needed to get clear of Swede. She knew that much. She just wasn't sure exactly how to do this without arousing his suspicions.

They returned to Lena's house, and she offered to put them up for the night.

Alexis sketched out a plan (kind of iffy, but it would have to do) for getting Swede and Lena to leave. Then she could slip out without anyone noticing.

"So, what's our next move?" Swede said. He seemed jumpy and irritable. Well, why wouldn't he be? Alexis thought.

"I . . . I'd like to spend a little time alone, if you don't mind." Alexis gave Swede her most entreating look. "I was just going to spend some time looking at his pictures and things. I guess I'm not quite done mourning yet." She laughed at herself, more in self-deprecation than humor.

Lena placed a hand on Swede's shoulder and threw Alexis a knowing look. "I'll leave the photo albums out. Swede and I will go somewhere else for a while, okay, kiddo?" She tugged at Swede's arm. "March, soldier," she said.

If Swede were a soldier, he looked about ready to go AWOL. However, Lena's persistent pull turned him away, resembling a reluctant child being told to go to his room. She winked at Alexis behind his back. Alexis returned it, grinning like they had a girl-to-girl conspiracy going. Boy, did that make her feel like shit.

φφφ

After they left, Alexis immediately called her sister in New York.

"Allie?" Katie usually answered her work phone with her own name, but she must have seen Alexis' cell number on the caller ID. Katie sounded almost breathless, as if expecting the worst.

"Yeah, it's me, Katie. I need to see you about something Daniel left with you?" Her statement ended as a question.

A brief silence, then Katie said, "Can I ask you a question?"

"Sure."

Another pause, then Katie spoke. "Do you remember the vacation we took to Jackson Hole as kids?"

"Uh . . . yeah." Alexis wondered where this was leading.

"Remember the secret I told you?"

Alexis racked her brain. She did recall something, but what was it? "That was ages ago. Hang on." Then it came to her. "Wasn't it about your crush on that boy who worked at McDonald's?"

Alexis heard Katie exhale at the other end. "Okay. I know this is weird, but I just wanted to be sure it was actually you. I mean it sounds like you . . . so I'm hoping this really *is* you." Her voice was tinged with desperation.

"Yes, Katie. It's really me. What's wrong?"

Katie issued a shuddering breath. "Daniel did give me some papers. He told me to keep them in a completely safe place. He also said the strangest thing."

"What?"

"He said that if anything ever happened to him, I should wait for *you* to get in touch with *me* about them. Daniel was firm on that point. He warned me not to look at the papers or tell anyone else about them, because it could be dangerous. He said that he'd leave instructions for you. Well, I didn't know what to think, but he insisted it would all be fine, as long as you personally handled the matter."

"Why me?" Alexis said it more to herself than Katie.

"How should I know? Daniel was always so secretive. Is this about his work?"

"No!" Alexis blurted. "I mean, I don't know." She tried to modify her tone. "So, looks like I need to come out there and personally handle the matter-- whatever that is. Could I stay with you?"

"Of course!" Katie said. "I'd love to see you. Don't you have any idea what this is all about?"

Alexis toyed with how much to tell Katie. She worked for a big publisher. Alexis knew she probably had contacts all throughout the business who'd be interested in getting a story out of this. Daniel had told her not to tell anyone what she was doing. Alexis sucked in her breath. Surely this couldn't include Katie, too. Or could it?

"I believe it may be something . . . involving an old friend, but I'm not sure," Alexis said. She felt like she was playing chess.

"Well . . . okay," Katie said. "But, c'mon. It must be pretty big to bring you all the way out to New York."

"I'll tell you what I know when I get there, okay?"

"Alexis Sullivan, you are impossible. But if you insist." Katie sounded philosophical but disappointed. Alexis thought about just telling her and being done with it, but something held her back.

Daniel's note. Clearly, Daniel hadn't told Katie much of anything, since she was so curious.

"Great. Thanks. Oh, by the way, could you do me a favor?"

"Sure. What?"

"Can you arrange a flight from Portland to New York for me. Like today. As soon as possible."

Katie must have detected my anxiety. "What's going on, Allie?"

"I'm in a difficult situation, and I need to get out of here. Now."

Katie paused a moment. "Okay," she said, sounding stunned. "I'll need some information, so I can set it up."

"I can't thank you enough." Alexis glanced out the window and at the clock. Time to call a cab and get the hell out of there.

CHAPTER TWENTY-TWO

JESSICA

The sun was setting. I realized that my morning bagel and granola bar lunch weren't cutting it. I needed food now.

I saved my story, backed up my files, and shut down the laptop. I'd spotted a few restaurants, but I wasn't sure I wanted to go out. Room service would be more expensive but possibly safer.

Thinking of the extra cost as a form of insurance, I phoned down for a hamburger and side salad. The salad inflated the tab, but I really needed to eat something healthy. I didn't know how long I could afford to stay here or how many chances at a healthy meal I'd get in the days to come.

I turned the TV back on and paced, tossing glances out the window. The sun had slipped low enough to cast the street in blue-gray shadow. Commuters scrambled past each other on the sidewalks and intersections. Lighted windows scattered across the facade of a nearby office building. Cabs and cars and buses and trucks crawled through the street several stories below me like blood through clogged arteries.

I kept my ear tuned for news about me or Fred, but they were still going on about terrorist threats and Homeland

Security. I muted the sound and turned on the radio, continuing to pace as I watched the anchor speak to the sound of the Beatles singing "Help!" I couldn't have said it better myself.

A knock on the door brought me to a halt before I went to answer.

"Yes?"

"Room service," an accented voice said.

I opened the door with the chain still in place. A Hispanic-looking man with black uniform pants and a white jacket and shirt smiled at me from behind a rolling cart with a covered tray on it.

I closed the door to unlock the chain and reopened it. The man rolled the cart in and placed the tray on a desk. I lifted the lid, saw the burger and salad, and my stomach audibly rumbled.

I blushed, and the man smiled again. He handed me the bill, in a faux leather holder. But there was no pen.

"Got a pen?"

The man's grin widened. I noticed a gold incisor winking in the corner of his mouth. He spread his hands and looked confused.

"Sorry?"

"A pen. There must be one around here." I checked the desk. No pen. The side table had no pen, either. I dug through my purse, seeking anything to write with.

Something pressed against my mouth and nose and pulled my head back. A hand jammed something soft against my face. An acrid, medicinal smell burned my nostrils. I struggled to get free, and then everything went dark.

φφφ

I awoke sprawled across the bed, with a mild headache. I blinked, propped myself on one arm and looked around the room. My food was still on the table. I sucked in a quick breath and let it out when I saw my purse and laptop were still there.

"What the hell just happened?" I muttered. My throat felt raw and my voice had a raspy edge to it.

I sat up, causing the room to tilt momentarily. Pausing, I got my bearings back before venturing to my feet.

Room service. Who was that guy with the gold tooth? He must have used something to knock me out. Why? Hopefully, nothing had been stolen.

My gaze swerved back to my shoulder bag and laptop. I stumbled toward them, and the floor bucked beneath my feet. After checking to make sure the contents of each appeared unmolested, I turned toward the door. It was closed, but the deadbolt and chain weren't locked.

The room spun as I crossed it. I leaned against the door until the spinning stopped, then fumbled the locks into place.

Taking baby steps, I made my way toward the room service tray. The hamburger was cold. Not that I was hungry anymore.

Someone had shut the curtains, but I could detect a fine, dark line between them. It must be late. Or early. Slowly turning my head, I saw the bedside clock read 10:35. So, late then.

I heard the toilet flush. That's when I realized the bathroom door was closed. I heard movement within. I ran to the room service tray and grabbed a serrated knife provided with the silverware.

When the door opened, I thought I would scream. I opened my mouth, but nothing came out when I saw who it was.

"Jessica? Are you all right?"

"Cynthia." For a moment, her name just hung in the air between us. "What are you doing here?"

φφφ

Ten minutes later, I'd surreptitiously stowed the knife under a pillow and was still absorbing the explanation Cyn had offered. She claimed to have been worried enough after I disappeared from the restaurant to have checked with Shelley about whether she'd heard from me. Shelley had told her about my need to leave town because of a "family emergency." I was trying to remember if I'd ever mentioned to Shelley where I was going, while Cyn rattled on nonstop.

"When I saw on the news that Fred had been murdered, I just about freaked out! Then, your name came up and . . . well, I just couldn't believe you'd had anything to do with it." She stopped for breath, with her head bowed and looked up at me uncertainly. "You didn't, right?"

"Of course not! I could never do anything like that. What reason would I have?"

Cyn seemed to be watching me closely. I imagined my own look probably mirrored hers.

"By the way," I said. "How did you find me here?"

Cyn looked embarrassed. "I found your sister, actually. I saw you leave her place and followed the cab."

"Oh, okay." I tried to sound casual, but the wheels were turning in my mind. Why did that explanation seem a bit too pat? I mean, what a co-ink-a-dink. I happened to leave my sister's condo, and Cyn just happened to be outside her place and watched me leave. Coincidences do happen, but things were getting to be a little hard to believe.

"I told the guy at the desk I was a friend who was concerned about you, because you'd disappeared and all. He was very kind. Gave me your room number."

I nodded, wondering how much she'd paid for that information.

Cyn's eyes widened, and she thrashed the air with both hands as she spoke. "When I got here, the door was open! I knocked, but no one answered, so I walked right in.

"You were out cold on the bed, stretched sideways across it. I figured I'd wait for you to wake up, just to make sure you were okay. You must have been exhausted to fall asleep like that." She gave me a sharp look. "And what were you thinking, leaving your door open? You could have been robbed or . . . ." She shuddered. "Or worse."

"I know." I wondered how much to believe of her story. I'd gathered more strength as she'd told it, but my thinking was still a little fuzzy from whatever I'd been drugged with. Should I challenge her or just go along? Which was safer?

Wait a minute, I thought. This is Cynthia we're talking about. What would she have to do with anything? She was only a friend of Fred's. Or was she?

I didn't want to assume anything. But right now, I had two men—two men who might have killed Fred—following me all the way across the country and talking to my sister for reasons I couldn't begin to know. I had no idea who I could trust and who I couldn't. The notion of trust was becoming laughable.

"Well, fortunately, nothing happened." I left it at that.

"Thank God for that." Cyn leaned toward me and placed a hand on my arm. I almost recoiled. "Let's make sure it stays that way."

φφφ

Making the excuse that I could use some "alone time" to work on my novel (telling her I needed sleep seemed bizarre under the circumstances), I gently (but firmly) asked Cynthia if she'd mind continuing our talk in the morning. She smiled and nodded—Cyn was so good at that—and we made plans to get together for breakfast. She told me she was staying at a place only a block or two away. We exchanged cell numbers, at her insistence, and after a protracted farewell, I saw her out the door, quickly locking it behind her.

I briefly thought of switching hotels, but it was so late and I'd already had enough trouble finding one I could afford that wasn't a fleabag. Besides, if I was under someone's surveillance, what would stop them from simply following me to the next hotel? One that would only end up costing more and giving no benefit in return.

My mind reeled with possibilities. Did Cynthia know the two men? Could she and Liz both be in on this? (Whatever "this" was.) I shook my head and wandered over to my laptop.

This time, I registered something weird about the laptop. I could swear I'd left it right in front of the chair where I'd been working. But the laptop was placed at an angle not suitable for working. Why?

I sat down and pulled the laptop into position before me and pondered it. Did someone tamper with it?

I started it up and got a message—something about shutting down in the middle of running a program.

"Great. What's this?"

Perhaps whoever knocked me out went through my files. All my novel's chapters, my research notes, and whatever was in my browser's cache.

Then, I remembered Selby's words and thought, "Is all this really about the novel?"

That's crazy.

Fred wanted to tell me something important. Could it be the people who are after me think he actually succeeded in doing that?

CHAPTER TWENTY-THREE

JESSICA

I tried to remain calm and reason it out. What could Fred have wanted to tell me and how would it relate to the novel I was working on? It was just too bizarre to think that the people who were after me were like those who were after Alexis.

I shook my head, as I opened my word processing program. I wanted so much to finish my novel. But doing so meant rehashing all the horrible similarities between my life my work. *Am I writing a novel or a thinly veiled autobiography?* I laughed, but the sound was less happy than desperate.

If nothing else, it seemed wise to check my files and make sure nothing had been deleted. If my novel had been deleted, in whole or part, I'd need to find a geek to recover what was lost.

Resolutely, I turned to my laptop and scanned the chapters quickly to where I'd left off, after Alexis had slipped away from Swede and gone to New York.

φφφ

ALEXIS

Alexis arrived at LaGuardia, feeling frazzled and more than a little ill at ease. She wasn't sure whether to feel triumphant or like a heel for ditching Swede the way she did.

As she toted her bag off the plane, she looked around for someone carrying a sign with her name on it. Her sister Katie had arranged for a car to pick her up. It was coming up on midnight and Katie lived in Manhattan, where owning a car was a huge expense and an annoyance. However, Katie said she'd wait up for her.

A short, balding man in a suit and hat, with broad, liver-spotted features and tired eyes, awaited her with sign in hand. Alexis walked up.

"I'm Alexis Sullivan," she said.

"Oh, good." The little man said it like he meant entirely the opposite. "I'm Mel. I'm your drivah."

If Mel was any indication, New Yorkers weren't terribly effusive.

"Got everything?" Mel asked.

"Yup." Alexis could match his lack of effusiveness with her own brand of taciturn.

Mel just nodded and looked relieved. "Well, dis way den." Alexis followed.

φφφ

En route to Katie's place, Alexis and Mel exchanged few words at first. Alexis was too tired to think of anything to talk about, and Mel seemed happy with that.

As they crossed the Queensboro Bridge, Mel spoke up. "So, your first time in Noo Yawk?"

"Oh, no. I've been here before. My sister has lived here a while."

"Uh huh. Where you from?"

"I go to school in Eugene. University of Oregon."

"Or-e-gahn, huh?" Or that's how it sounded to Alexis. "Lotsa rain, I hear."

"Well, sometimes, but . . . ." She cut herself off. Oregonians wanted people to think it rains there all the time so they won't be overrun with transplanted East Coasters--Californians were more than enough to handle as it was. "But you get used to it," she finished.

Mel shook his head. "Can't abide rain awl the time. Brings me down, ya know?"

Alexis could just imagine how far down Mel was capable of going.

φφφ

Mel left Alexis at the door to Katie's Upper East Side condo. She hit the buzzer and a doorman in a regal maroon coat with gold epaulets let her in.

Alexis gave her name and started to say she was there to see Katie, but the doorman cut her off. "Ah, no worries," he said, with a faint Irish brogue. "Mrs. Wilson told me you'd be showing up any time. I'll be ringing her then, to let her know you're on your way."

Alexis wanted to correct the man, who apparently didn't know that Katie had legally resumed using her maiden name after her divorce, but she simply smiled and nodded instead. She assumed the condo directory still had her listed as Katherine Wilson.

The doorman ducked behind a marble-topped counter and picked up the receiver of a blinding white phone so shiny, Alexis wondered if the man spent his idle time polishing it. He punched in a number and dismissed her with a wave of his hand. "Go on, now. I'm just announcing you."

Alexis nodded again and turned toward the elevators. She could barely make out the doorman's voice as he muttered into the receiver. This didn't feel right. Alexis shrugged off the wave of anxiety. *Daniel's note must be putting my nerves on edge.*

An elevator opened, and a man and a woman were inside. Apparently, they'd come up from the parking garage below, but they didn't seem to be together. Alexis entered the elevator and hit the button for the fifteenth floor. She pulled out her phone and called Katie. When Katie answered, Alexis breathed a sigh of relief.

"Did the doorman just call you?" Alexis asked.

"Uh, yes. What's wrong?" Katie's voice. It didn't sound quite right.

"I might ask you the same question." Alexis glanced about her. The other passengers seemed to be listening to her. Ridiculous. It was just idle curiosity. After all, she was the only one doing any talking.

The elevator stopped on the ninth floor. The doors opened and the woman left. The man stayed on, averting his eyes from Alexis.

"I'm . . . fine," Katie said.

"Well, you don't sound like it."

A long pause ensued. The man kept looking everywhere except at Alexis. His hand moved into his coat pocket.

"Is there something you want to tell me?" Alexis asked. "Should I stay somewhere else tonight?"

Alexis kept the man in her peripheral vision. He fumbled in his coat pocket for a bit and pulled out a key. Alexis felt overcome with gratitude and embarrassment at assuming it was going to be a gun or knife or a drug-soaked rag.

Katie laughed, but not with any sort of glee. "Of course you can stay here. But that's entirely up to you."

This was completely wrong. Katie would never have said that. It was after midnight. She would have insisted Alexis spend the night with her. Somebody was with Katie, so she couldn't speak freely. And the doorman. He should've known her name. And he wouldn't have shooed Alexis away like that, unless he had something to hide.

The elevator reached the fifteenth floor, emitting a bell-like chime as it did. Alexis and the man emerged and, as she headed toward the stairs, she heard him say, "Stop right there, miss."

She stopped and turned with almost glacial slowness toward him. He held up the key. "Come with me."

Alexis stood paralyzed, rooted in place for a moment. Then, she turned and bolted for the exit stairs. She glanced back at the man as she threw open the door and just before she ran into the stairwell, she saw him pounding toward her, pulling a small walkie-talkie from his coat pocket.

Alexis may have spent a lot of time in the library, but she kept fit. Oregon had lots of places to hike, a passion for both Daniel and herself. She bounded down the steps, taking them two at a time. The man pursuing her seemed to have substantial difficulty keeping up. The distance between them was growing greater with each flight, but Alexis knew that the test would be whether she could lose the man after she left the stairwell.

She reached the lobby and tried to open the door. Locked. Frantic, Alexis raced down to the next level and tried the door. It wouldn't budge. She'd reached the bottom. No way out, at least none that she could see. She could hear the man from the elevator getting closer.

Alexis pounded on the door. "Open up!" she yelled.

The man's footsteps were getting louder, and she pounded harder.

"Help! Anyone there?"

The door flew open and, in it, stood Mel.

"C'mon, kid." He grabbed her arm, pulled her into the garage and slammed the door. Mel hustled Alexis toward the car, pushed her into the passenger's side. She flopped onto the seat like a ragdoll. Mel shut the door, hurried round to the driver's side, started up the car and left the garage with a squeal of tires.

φφφ

JESSICA

I stopped scanning pages to take a break. When I'd first written these words, they'd poured onto the page in such a rush, I was sure they'd prove upon later inspection to be a bunch of crap. But they felt right somehow, possibly because Alexis' situation (even though it was fictional) seemed worse than my own.

Mel had surprised me. A minor character had suddenly grabbed the spotlight. Don't ask me why. He just did. Somehow it seemed to fit.

I felt chilly and a bit light-headed, as if re-reading and reliving these words in my head had been like vomiting. Or maybe it was just having been drugged and being up after midnight.

And, if I'd been looking for solutions in my writing, they were still eluding me.

I turned on the TV again, hoping to find a good movie to help lull me to sleep so my body could regain the proper circadian rhythm.

As I flipped through the channels, I once again hit CNN and stopped briefly to see if I were being featured. Instead, I saw a photo of the Golden Gate Bridge and heard the news anchor say they were closing it as a precaution against a purported threat.

CHAPTER TWENTY-FOUR

KEVIN

He rubbed his hands with glee. Jessica had no idea what she was up against. And neither did the authorities.

Selby's death had been unfortunate but unavoidable. Nonetheless, the group had the benefit of his knowledge, so his death didn't really matter. A huge disaster was in the works. The group's operatives were doing a masterful job of misdirecting everyone, sending the FBI and CIA chasing their own tails, like cats on cocaine. And Homeland Security was equally clueless.

Wait 'til they find out what's really up, he thought. And little did they know, the clock was ticking. Just as it was for Kevin.

CHAPTER TWENTY-FIVE

JESSICA

My first thought was of Mom and Dad. They lived in the bedroom community of San Rafael and often ventured into San Francisco. The Golden Gate Bridge would be the most logical way in for them.

It must have been a serious threat for the authorities to shut down the bridge. There were other bridges one could take, but the route was substantially longer. And the traffic would be a commuter nightmare. The ferries would make out well.

Fortunately, my Dad could telecommute and Mom worked as a librarian at the College of Marin in Kentfield, so she didn't have to cross the bridge. I was grateful for that, plus the fact that San Rafael is 30 miles north of the city.

I changed the channel quickly, trying to put the matter out of mind. I already had enough to worry about. I didn't need to dwell on disasters that might befall my parents.

After a time, I finally landed on a channel with a movie. An old one, from the looks of it. I turned the sound low enough to hear it, but soft enough so it wouldn't keep me from drifting off. Eventually, I did just that.

I woke to hear the phone ringing. It felt like I'd been asleep for only ten minutes, but the light shining through the crack in the curtains told me otherwise.

I picked up. "Hullo," I croaked.

"Jessica? It's me."

It took a moment to register who "me" was. "Hi Cyn. I guess it's breakfast time, huh?"

"Jessica, what have you done?"

Those words jolted me awake. "Huh?" I said. "I explained about finding Fred, right?"

"This isn't about Fred. I'm talking about that man yesterday. Who was he?"

"Uh." I was stumped momentarily, then did a mental head smack. Selby. Shit.

"The man at Navy Memorial. It's all over the local news."

Good God. How many more people were going to see me fleeing murder scenes? According to my research, eye witness testimony is so unreliable. Yet, here I was being identified all over the country.

The TV was still on, so I grabbed the remote and flipped through channels until I found a local station. They had a morning show going, so I'd have to wait until they switched to local news or just check the morning paper and see if I'd ended up being featured on page one above the fold. That seemed unlikely given that this was the Nation's Capital, which was also homicide central. Yet a murder in a crowd at the Navy Memorial in broad daylight might get a bit more attention than usual. Needless to say, I wasn't thrilled.

"Are you going to tell me what happened?"

I'd forgotten about Cynthia. "It's not the way it looks, okay?" I paused to collect myself, before launching into an explanation of the strange phone calls, the two men in the van and my decision to come to D.C. Then the call from the stranger, the meeting, the poisoning and—worst of all—seeing my sister with Flattop and Red.

"Okay, so you lied to your adviser," Cyn said. "There's no family emergency. How am I supposed to believe what you've told me about Fred?"

"Why would I kill Fred?"

A protracted silence followed. "Fair enough, but it really looks suspicious. And now this latest murder. I mean, what the hell is going on?"

"If you only knew how many times I've asked myself that same question."

"Look, you stay there and I'll bring you something to eat."

I sighed. "That's probably a good idea. I don't need yet another person recognizing me. Apparently, my face is more memorable than most."

"It was probably that silly hat."

"Could be." I had to admit, in retrospect, it did seem ridiculous. My stomach growled and I realized I was famished. I'd had only a bagel and the granola bar yesterday. I'd left the room service food untouched. "Well, whatever. I'm starving."

"All right, then. I'll pick up coffee and some cinnamon rolls."

"That'll be fine. Thanks."

I hung up and kept my eye on the TV, watching for any news about me or yesterday's murder. I flipped around to more local stations. Nothing. Maybe it was already old news.

Then, on one channel, I saw the photo they'd shown of me on CNN. I turned up the sound.

" . . . witness noticed Evans talking to the man moments before he was found dead. At that time, Evans wore jeans, a blue T-shirt, and a hat. Police are asking that you call them if you see Evans, the woman in this photo."

Super. I muted the sound and pondered the strange ways of fate.

Then, I wondered about the description the anchorwoman had given. Apparently, no one had taken a photo of me at the Navy Memorial, or you'd think they would've used it instead of the one from CNN. The anchorwoman had also mentioned what I wore but never described the hat and it was pretty distinctive.

I'd left the hat back at Liz's condo before I took the cab to my hotel. Cynthia had told me she saw me leave Liz's place, but never mentioned seeing me arrive. So how would she know about the hat?

CHAPTER TWENTY-SIX

JESSICA

The knock at the door had to be Cyn. I grabbed the serrated knife and opened the door with the chain in place.

"I bring breakfast." Cyn's cheery greeting could be heard on the next floor.

I unlocked the chain and opened the door. Cyn entered with a paper bag. "These cinnamon rolls look absolutely sinful," she said. "Better be hungry or I'll gain a ton eating them." She moved to small desk and pulled coffee cups and pastry from the bag.

"Cyn?" Her false bonhomie was wearisome. "How did you know about my hat?"

Cyn hesitated a fraction of a second. "It was on the news."

"Which channel?"

"I'm not sure. CNN, maybe."

"And why did you follow me here again?"

Cyn turned toward me, looking put out. "Why all the questions?"

"They're easy ones. Or should be."

She shook her head. "I'm not allowed to be concerned about you?"

I sighed and turned away. *What did I just ask? Why aren't you answering?*

That's when I noticed the door was ajar.

I grabbed Cyn from behind, jamming the serrated edge of the knife against her throat. She emitted an audible gasp and swept a coffee cup to the floor. Coffee seeped out, its dark stain spreading out across the carpet.

"The door's unlocked. Why?" I snarled.

"Please!" Her voice came out in ragged gasps. "I didn't mean to do it."

"Really?" My voice took on a mock saccharine tone. "You're so concerned for me, you follow me across the country, but you leave my hotel room unlocked. That does not compute."

"Okay, okay," Cyn said. "I can explain."

"Then start explaining." I pressed the knife harder. "Now!"

Cyn caught her breath. "Can you take that knife away from my throat first?"

"Sorry. Given the past few days events, my faith in human nature is wavering a bit."

Cyn seemed to consider this. "All right, then. It's like this."

In an instant, she grabbed my wrist, pulled it from her throat and twisted my arm behind my back.

As I struggled, two men came in and grabbed me. Once they had me in their grasp, Cyn stood before me. She hauled back and slapped my face.

"Bitch!" I said, spit flying with my words. "Did you kill Fred?"

"I don't think you're in a position to ask questions, dear." Cyn's voice fairly dripped with sarcasm. Gone was the whole bubble-headed blonde act. Her expression had turned glacial. There was clearly much more to her than met the eye.

I kicked out at her, but she stepped out of reach. My captors clamped onto my arms like pit bulls.

"Keep hold of her," Cyn said. "And watch her fucking feet." She turned and left the room.

For a moment, no one said anything. The two men still dug their fingers into my arms.

"Now what?" I asked. I tried to sound tough, but my voice was shaking. I wasn't sure if it was because of fear or anger.

"Now, we make you talk." One of the men smiled at me the way a shark might smile at a minnow.

"That's nice. What shall we talk about?"

The man's smile morphed into a scowl. He leaned in so his face was an inch from mine. I could smell the mints he used in a lame attempt to cover his coffee-and-cigarette breath.

"What . . . did . . . he . . . tell . . . you?" He enunciated the words slowly, as if I were a child or an idiot. Or someone who'd just learned English. Each word brought another mint-laced blast of stink breath.

My first thought was, "Who? Fred or Selby?" But since neither had told me anything, I said, "Nobody has told me anything!"

The man smiled again. He looked me up and down. His eyes brightened and his nostrils flared.

"We'll see how much you know, baby." He leaned in as his buddy grabbed my other arm and held both behind my back. Then, he jammed his stinky-breathed mouth against mine. He forced his tongue inside my mouth and down to my tonsils. It took everything I had to keep from gagging, not only from his breath but also from his ridiculously long tongue.

He started moaning and grinding his pelvis against me. There was no mistaking his intentions now.

At this point, my knowledge of self-defense kicked into high gear. He stopped a moment and stepped back just far enough for me to jab my knee up into his groin. He fell back and doubled over in pain.

The man behind me dug his fingers in harder. I brought my foot up and smashed it down on his instep. He screamed and his fingers loosened. An elbow jab to the gut moved him back enough to let me karate chop his groin. As he bent over, I used his momentum to throw him to the floor. At which point, I stomped on his head.

I started for the door, then sprinted to the table, snatched my flash drive, and ran. But not before breaking both men's noses with a swift kick to each of their faces.

Did I just kick two men in the face? Did I really just break their noses? For a moment, as I fled toward the stairwell—checking the door before entering to make sure I wouldn't end up trapped like Alexis—I actually felt a pang of guilt. *I'm not a violent person. But that man was going to rape me. And I don't think the other guy intended to stop him. So, what the hell do I have to feel guilty about?*

I bounded down the stairs as fast as I could go, wondering where the hell I was going.

It seemed to take forever to reach each landing. My room was on the eighth floor and I counted down each floor every two flights. Seven . . . six . . . five . . . .

I reached floor two and paused. Maybe I should get out here. Just in case. I tried the knob. It turned. I pushed through the door. It opened into a hall. The elevators were located to my left in an alcove midway down the hall. As I ran toward the alcove, a man rounded the corner. Another man followed. It was Flattop and Red—the men from the van. I skidded to a halt and scrambled to switch directions.

"Wait!" Flattop caught up with me in short order and grabbed my arm, then eased off with surprising gentleness. "We work for your sister. And we're here to protect you."

CHAPTER TWENTY-SEVEN

JESSICA

My mouth must have resembled that of a landed grouper. My lips kept flapping, but I couldn't find the words.

"What?" Sadly, it was the most intelligent thing I could think of to say.

Flattop smiled and reached into his back pocket. I tensed, then relaxed, feeling stupid as he pulled out a wallet and opened it.

He handed me a card. It read *Joseph Cotter, A-Team Security*.

I gaped at the card, until I finally found my voice again, hiding somewhere beneath my liver. "Wait. Are you telling me my sister hired you as my bodyguard?"

Flattop (or Cotter, if that *was* his name) nodded. "Your sister gave us the okay to tell you. She knew you were caught in something bigger than you could imagine."

"Hold on," I said. "A couple of people have died." I waved the card under his nose. "I need more than this to be convinced. Anyone can have business cards made up."

Cotter frowned. "I'm sorry. Will this do it?" He opened his wallet again and displayed his driver's license, then flipped to a card that showed he was state-certified in California as a bodyguard.

"I . . . I have to call my sister," I said, my voice faint with disbelief.

"Go ahead. But I think we need to get you out of here."

As Cotter and his redhead assistant led me further down the stairs, I was able to reach Liz on my cell.

"Jess! Are you okay?" Her voice sounded tight with near panic.

"I'm okay." For a moment, I thought I'd burst into tears but I struggled to contain myself. "Well, that's a lie. I feel like shit. I met my bodyguards, by the way."

"Jess, I hired them to make sure no one hurt you."

We had clambered down to a basement garage and my bodyguards hustled me toward a car. (Like Alexis. Not again!)

"Just so I'm sure, tell me their names."

"Joe Cotter and Billy Sullivan."

Billy Sullivan? Now, how weird was that? My protagonist Alexis' surname was Sullivan. This had to be a bad dream. They say truth is stranger than fiction, but honestly . . . this was way too much.

"Okay," I said, sliding into the back, while Cotter and Billy took their places up front. I breathed a sigh of relief, knowing that Liz had actually hired these guys. However, I still had a few questions for her.

"So, exactly why do I need to be guarded?" I asked, settling back in the seat and wishing I could feel as relaxed as that pose.

"I'll explain everything after the guys bring you in."

"Bring me in?" I asked. "Where?"

"The safe house."

Although the words "safe house" made me feel anything but, I tried to relax during our ride out of town. As we drove, I asked Cotter, "Well, if you're my bodyguards, where the hell have you been all this time?"

"Your sister called a meeting with us yesterday. Shortly after you arrived at the Navy Memorial. I told her we were watching you, but she seemed to feel you'd be safe there. She was anxious to meet with us out of your view and discuss the latest developments with us. She's the client, so we had our meeting."

"What about him? Couldn't you have left him to watch me?" I gestured toward Billy, who looked back at me with an open expression and slightly goofy grin that seemed to answer my own question.

Cotter shook his head. "Too green." Based on appearances, I had to agree.

"So, you had nothing to do with either Fred or Selby's death?"

"Of course not. We went back to the memorial after our meeting. We couldn't find you there, so we returned to our surveillance post down the street from your sister's building. You must have slipped out while our backs were turned."

"Then how the heck did you find my hotel?"

Cotter glanced up at me in the rear view. His eyes were cagey, but kindness lurked beneath the steeliness.

"Your sister came home after work. She flipped out when she saw that you and your things were gone. She's been worried sick and feeling guilty for calling us off the guard detail."

I nearly admitted that I'd freaked out and caused my own problems after seeing the two of them with my sister, but held my tongue.

"Anyhow, after that, we were authorized to do an all-out search for you. One of our strategies was to call cab companies. It took a lot of phoning and a bit of cash." Here, Cotter held up a hand and rubbed his fingers together. "But we were able to find out from the right cab company's records when and where you went. Took us all night, but by God, we did it." Cotter sounded proud and even a little emotional about this achievement.

We drove out to a brick rancher on a tree-lined rollercoaster of a street called Dale Drive in the Maryland suburbs. As I emerged from the car, Liz came running out to meet me.

We hugged so hard, I thought she'd squeeze the tears right out of me.

"I'm so sorry," Liz said. "I didn't want to tell you for fear of worrying you."

Tell me what? my mind shrieked. But I was too tired for hysterics.

"Liz, please tell me what this is about." I sounded pathetic.

Liz insisted we go inside to discuss it. Once inside, Liz put some coffee on and produced some deli sandwiches. I nearly pounced on them, since I hadn't eaten a thing in almost 24 hours.

I unwrapped and tore into a turkey sandwich. "This is delicious," I said, around a mouthful of sandwich.

"Got 'em at Ertter's, right down the road," Liz said.

I chewed and swallowed, holding off on the next bite out of sheer force of will. "It's been too long since we last saw each other, Liz. But this is one fucked up reunion."

Liz's lips compressed into a wry smile. "You're telling me."

"So, just what is going on?"

Liz sighed. "Homeland Security contacted me. They knew about the extremist group, because of a mole."

"Selby?"

She shook her head. "I don't know. They don't tell me everything. They're very good at telling me just enough, without telling it all."

She poured two cups of coffee and brought them to the table, along with some milk and sugar, then sat across from me.

"All I know is that they heard from their source that the group was planning a big incident. Something so catastrophic, it could surpass 9/11."

I stopped eating and peered at her. She was dead serious.

"The mole found out that the fellow who was doing research for you was giving you information," she continued. "They assumed it was for your book."

"Yes," I said, my voice weighted with guilt. "I think he died trying to help me out. So, is the group really working on a weapon more powerful than an atom bomb?"

Liz frowned and her eyebrows dueled briefly with one another. "Is that what your book is about?"

"Well, yes, it's a thriller about a scientist who's researching a theory that Einstein was wrong, that the speed of light is variable, and that under his new theory, it's possible to build a weapon many times stronger than the H-bomb. The scientist dies under suspicious circumstances. It's supposed to be an accident. Blah, blah, blah. Never mind all that. Is that what the group is doing?"

Liz raised a finger. "That's the thing, Jess. We don't know. Homeland Security only knows this radical group is worried about you. The group must have killed Fred, thinking he was passing you information about their plans."

"Well, the cops haven't gotten that memo, have they? They think I did it."

She shook her head. "No, they were told to issue that statement. They wanted to take you into protective custody without revealing their plans to the group."

I opened my mouth, but only a guttural sound of disbelief came out, at first. "So all this time, I thought I was a murder suspect and I wasn't?" *Those assholes!*

Liz looked ready to cry. "I wanted to tell you, but I couldn't. Attorney-client privilege. I'm only telling you this now, because the Feds want your cooperation."

My jaw dropped and, for a moment, I stared at her. "What?"

"Jessica, I wouldn't ask if it weren't essential. And we're talking about a huge catastrophe. Who knows how big."

I managed to close my mouth and gather my wits. "Does this have anything to do with the situation at the Golden Gate Bridge?"

"Possibly."

"That's it? That's all you can say?"

"It's all we know, Jess. Really!" Liz stared off, looking almost as dazed as I was. But that wasn't going to deter me from probing further, because the whole thing smelled fishy to me.

"If it affects the Bay Area and it's that catastrophic, how come they aren't evacuating San Francisco?"

Liz reared up and glared at me, as if I'd hurled an insult at her. "I told you it was only a possibility. We can't go causing a general panic based on a mere possibility. That's why the Feds need your help."

I sighed and asked, "What do they want from me?"

Liz hesitated and then said, "They want to use you in a sting operation."

CHAPTER TWENTY-EIGHT

JESSICA

I stared at Liz in disbelief. "You must be joking, right? Tell me you're joking. I mean you can't possibly be serious. No way, no way. You *can't* be serious!" The more I spoke, the faster my words came and the more hysterical I sounded.

Liz wouldn't return my look. She propped her elbows on the table and kneaded her temples with both hands. "None of this is my idea, Jess. I don't like it any more than you do. I haven't liked *any* of this." Her voice dripped with disgust.

"Oh, yeah. Well, I've been enjoying it even less, okay? So you and your goddamned federal government can just kiss my ass!"

Liz stopped kneading long enough to venture a look my way. Her eyes were tired, pleading with me for understanding. "It's your government, too, Jessica. And this catastrophe could kill hundreds of millions of innocent people."

"Hundreds of millions?"

Liz leaned toward me. "Would you believe entire countries?"

I was silent for a beat. "What kind of catastrophe could do that?"

"One involving a bomb like the one in your book maybe?"

I nodded. "Okay, but I don't go into all the scientific details. I don't even talk about how the bomb could be built. It's all theory, and it's not even accepted theory in the real world. Are you sure this catastrophe relates to my novel?"

"Well, Fred was killed helping you research it. Then Selby was killed and he knew Fred."

I tried to think back to my meeting with Selby. Something he'd said. He'd told me Fred was killed because of something related to the novel, but he also said the group was relying on something he knew.

"What was Selby's major?" I muttered aloud.

"Hmm?"

"I'm trying to remember what Selby studied. I wonder if Fred ever mentioned it."

"Was it physics? Or chemistry?"

"I . . . I don't know. It had to be a science of some sort, now that I think about it. I remember when we met on campus, Selby mentioned his research. But if it was physics, I would remember that because I was so interested in finding out more about João Magueijo's theory. I'm sure I would have asked him about it. If I could just remember . . . ."

A dark-haired man in a dark suit, blinding white shirt, and dark glasses glided into the kitchen, quiet as a church mouse. A woman who could have been his sister in a nearly matching skirted version of his suit stood just behind him, also wearing dark glasses. The Bobbsey Twins of the FBI. Or CIA. Or Homeland Security. Or whatever.

"Decision time," the man said, looking at me. At least his face was pointed my way.

"Who the hell are you guys?" I asked the well-dressed eavesdroppers.

"Agent Owen." He whipped out a badge, then waved a hand toward his female counterpart. "My associate and I work for Homeland Security."

"How nice for you." The response seemed ludicrous, but then so did the situation.

Liz looked defeated. "Jess, they want you to wear a wire and try to confirm our theories about these people. Will you do it?"

The word "no" was poised on the tip of my tongue, but I couldn't bring myself to say it. If hundreds of millions (and maybe billions) of lives were at stake, how could I say no to this? How could I just refuse and walk away?

"You see," Agent Owen said, as if the matter needed further elucidation. "You're in a unique position. They think you may have information about their plans. If we let them capture you and you can confirm exactly what they're up to, it could prevent the worst from happening."

He removed his dark glasses and I was surprised to see such friendly brown eyes behind them.

"If you pretend to help them, we don't think they'll hurt you. Pretend to be on their side, even, and try to draw them out. Meanwhile, we'll be monitoring everything that's said. And we won't let them harm you. I can assure you of that."

I opened my mouth, but the words seem to stick in my throat. I swallowed and tried again. "Two guys just tried to rape me. Then, I kicked them in the face. How will I convince them that I'm on their side? And how do I know they won't hurt me?"

Agent Owen took a deep breath, as if the inhalation could clarify his thought processes. He pursed his lips and nodded. "I think it can be arranged."

"Arranged how?"

"We have our ways." He made a placating, palms-down gesture with both hands. "The main thing is to try to get *any* information that could give us a better idea of their true intentions. Anything that will help us prevent a catastrophe and keep our operative safe."

"Operative?" My brows drew together. Even Liz looked at the man in alarm. "Wait a second. If you have an operative in the group, what the hell do you need me for?"

"Our operative has come under scrutiny. This operative could be completely compromised by asking the wrong questions. If that happened, the operative would be killed and months of work would be wasted. We'd be completely screwed."

"Who is this operative?" I asked. Liz's ears seemed to perk up, too.

Owen shook his head. "Need to know only."

CHAPTER TWENTY-NINE

JESSICA

"Oh, really?" I said, rising from my seat. "Well, guess what, buddy? I need to know and I need to know fucking now!"

Agent Owen looked at me askance and his female counterpart lurched to attention. Liz jumped up and placed herself between me and the man, as if to protect him from a physical attack.

"Sorry," the man said from behind Liz. "We aren't allowed to reveal that information."

I placed my hands on the table and leaned on them, taking deep breaths and counting to ten. Then twenty.

"Call us if you need us," Owen said to Liz. "We'll be in the other room." He started to go, and then stopped. "You need to decide quickly, Ms. Evans. Time is of the essence. And there's a lot at stake." With that, he and his twin partner high-tailed it out of there.

I sat back down and put my face in my hands.

"Why, Liz? Why did I have to write a thriller?"

I could hear Liz resume her seat across from me.

"Why couldn't I have just written, I don't know, romantic suspense?" I continued. "You know, one of those silly stories where Colonel Peacock gets killed in the garden with a hoe or a pitchfork and the heroine gets her man? Terrorist groups don't give a shit about those stories, do they?"

"Jessica, I'm so sorry. About everything." Liz sighed before continuing. "You have no idea how I've worried since Homeland Security told me all this. That's why I hired those guards. I wanted to protect you, and I hoped it wouldn't come to this. But, you do need to decide. And he's right. This could happen any time. So the sooner you decide, the more likely we are to prevent what may be the worst catastrophe in modern history."

"Shit." I stared into my hands, wishing I would wake up from this horrible dream. I briefly thought of all the films I'd seen in which the needs of one were outweighed by the needs of many. *Casablanca, Star Trek: Wrath of Khan.* Ugh, why do I watch movies or care about anything? My heart felt like a lead weight in my chest as I finally spoke. "What choice do I have? If they absolutely need me, I'll do it."

Even as I said it, I couldn't believe those words were coming from me.

Liz put her hand on my arm. "I . . . " She couldn't go on. After a few moments, she steeled herself and rose. "I'll go tell them." She turned and left the room. I almost shouted for her to wait, that I'd changed my mind, but the words wouldn't come. So I simply stared at her retreating back.

I had one night at the safe house, while plans were prepared for me to be kidnapped. Super, I thought. I wondered what delightful method they'd use. Would I be forced into a car at gunpoint or simply bashed over the head?

Agent Owen (whom I'd mentally dubbed George Clooney, because Owen and Clooney could've been brothers) told me not to worry, because the operative would do everything possible to make sure my capture was swift and painless. "Swift and painless"—words that could also apply to someone's death. Coming from good old George, I wasn't taking much comfort in them.

CHAPTER THIRTY

KEVIN

Kevin snapped out of his latest drug-induced haze and tried to focus on the problems at hand.

So the writer had gotten away and grievously wounded two of the group's men. But he knew it was just a matter of time before they flushed her out again. Then, they could ask her how much Fred had told her.

Fred's research for this woman had made him far too curious about other matters. Matters the woman could definitely confirm by talking to Selby.

While Selby was no longer a threat, the question was how much had he told her at their meeting?

The group's plans hinged on Selby's knowledge of a risk so little known, yet so potentially lethal, it was astonishing.

CHAPTER THIRTY-ONE

JESSICA

That night at the safe house, I thrashed around in bed, unable to sleep. Couldn't imagine why.

The room was hot and dusty, little-used, and unkempt with only a bed, a desk, a computer, and a bookshelf along one wall. The musty smell of old books made me feel like I was trying to sleep in the back room of a used book warehouse.

After 1:00 in the morning, I threw off the covers and got up. I peered through the Venetian blinds at the quiet, dark neighborhood. Everyone tucked safely in bed and sound asleep, no doubt. Or curled up in front of a television watching a late night movie and munching on popcorn or drinking cocoa.

If any of them had insomnia, it wasn't because they'd been called upon to be kidnapped by terrorists in order to help authorities save the world from its biggest catastrophe ever. Nor had they seen a nice guy like Fred lying on the floor with a bullet through his head. Or witnessed a man keel over dead—probably poisoned. And Cynthia of all people was involved with this group. Jesus!

All of this had started on Monday. Only a few days ago. Talk about your bad weeks. And it was just barely Friday.

I turned away from the window. Sleep was hopeless at this point. I could read a book. I scanned the titles. *Moby Dick? The Sound and the Fury?* I shook my head. No, thank you, limited edition or not. Desperate to keep my mind busy, I turned to my laptop. I sat at the desk and booted it up. No Internet access—something told me that was no accident.

My thoughts wandered to the story. Mel's appearance (plus the doorman's duplicity) had put a new wrinkle in things. I originally hadn't planned on Mel doing much, but now I decided to write a version in which he stepped to the fore.

This made me ponder the nature of choice. The many choices we're faced with every day. How do we choose what to do? Can we choose who we are? Or is that choice already made for us? Are our choices shaped by who we are? Or are we defined by our choices?

Here I was sitting in a dark bedroom, in a dark neighborhood, unable to sleep because of my choices. I'd chosen to serve my country rather than run away. Now, all I had to do was make a choice about my story. Or have my characters make their choices, because that's what it came down to.

The eerie similarities between my life and Alexis' life made me wonder if I'd subconsciously created my own situation. Perhaps the answers to why I was in my situation were right there in the words of my book. If a terrorist group was after me because my manuscript threatened them, maybe reviewing it would give me a clue as to how to extricate myself.

With that faint hope in mind, I plugged in the flash drive and opened the document again.

φφφ

ALEXIS

Alexis was barely able to catch her breath by the time the car squealed out of the garage.

"Who are you?" she gasped.

"A friend." Mel seemed disinclined to say more, which was completely consistent with their dealings so far, but Alexis was too curious to leave it at that.

"Care to explain? Are you Katie's friend or what?"

"I'm what you'd call an interested party."

Alexis noticed his thick New York accent had lightened. It was still there, just not quite as heavy. "Interested in what?" she asked, fearful at what he might answer.

"Alexis, when you called Katie and told her you were coming, we intercepted your call."

"What?"

Mel paused, as if gathering the strength to go on. "The federal government has been aware of the research done by your fiancé and Alan Sweetser for some time now. We've been watching them to see what they did with it."

Alexis nodded. "So, those guys Swede was talking about. They're with the Feds?"

"No." The word landed between them like a ten-ton anvil. "Terrorists groups have been interested in their research, too. The people who first approached them weren't with us."

"And who would you be with? FBI? CIA? What?"

"Ever hear of the NSA?"

The National Security Agency. Or, as it was once known, No Such Agency. Kind of a joke at one time, when a person who worked there couldn't even admit their own employer existed. But now everyone knew about the NSA, even if its employees couldn't talk about what they did. Even if they answered their phones with extension numbers instead of names. However, Alexis couldn't help but notice he hadn't actually answered her question.

"So, you work for the NSA?" she said.

"Didn't I just say that?"

"No, you didn't. And you haven't told me who those people are who have my sister or where the hell we're going or anything!" Alexis' voice broke with frustration. "Please, just give me a straight answer."

"All right." Alexis heard enough regret in Mel's stoic tone to suggest he was sorry, even if he wouldn't say the words. "Yes, I work at the NSA or Fort Meade, our latest euphemism. We intercepted your phone call. But someone must be telling the opposition. Somehow, they knew you'd be coming here and got to your sister before you did."

Alexis started to ask why he'd almost let her walk into a trap, but Mel held up a hand and continued talking.

"We let you go up to your sister's to keep from letting on that we knew."

"I see. So you let me almost walk into the arms of terrorists, just so your cover wouldn't be blown? Nice." Alexis hurled the last word out like a smash shot.

"Put yourself in our shoes, Alexis. What purpose would it serve to blow the operation when we're this close to catching these guys?"

Alexis sighed. They turned onto a bridge and the silence between them was filled with the whine of tires on metal grating.

Alexis found the noise hypnotic, as was the periodic whump, whump, whump as the car ran over connections between the grates.

"So, what now?" she asked.

"We have a mission."

Alexis snorted. "We? Since when did I join your merry band of spies?"

"Let's put it this way," Mel said, raising his voice over the road noise. "Your sister's in the hands of a group of terrorists, but apparently hasn't told them anything. With any luck, they won't torture her to find Daniel's papers, with or without your help."

Alexis gasped. "Oh, my God."

"Don't worry." Mel dismissed the torture scenario a bit too fast for Alexis' comfort. "Thing is, we could call in some heavy hitters with guns, but that could get ugly. We couldn't guarantee your sister's safety. You, on the other hand, could get to the papers without incident. Now, would you rather do that with or without our help?"

"Well, obviously with it." Alexis paused. "Not that I have much choice . . . ."

Her words trailed off. The car hit the pavement again, plunging them into a thick, uncomfortable silence.

"I guess we're partners whether I like it or not," Alexis said.

Mel's lips curled up in mild amusement. "You catch on fast."

Mel took Alexis to a small brick house in Queens. He grabbed her bag, hustled her through a gate in a waist-high chain link fence and into the cramped building.

The living room had only a sofa, TV set, and freestanding lamp that looked like they'd been picked up at a rummage sale.

"This is nice. Who's your decorator?" Alexis said.

Mel grunted. "Funny. They say laughter is the best medicine."

"I'd like to give you at taste of your own medicine," Alexis muttered between clenched teeth. Mel either didn't hear or chose to ignore her.

He led her down a short hallway, past a couple of closed doors to a small bedroom. He flipped on the overhead light which revealed a single bed made up with sheets, pillow, and blanket.

"Rest up," he said. "We'll talk about our strategy in the morning."

And with that, he shut the door. Alexis looked around the tiny room, feeling like a prisoner.

Too weary to bother with pajamas, Alexis stripped to her undies and dived under the covers.

It was approaching 2:30 A.M., when she woke as the doorknob turned with a metallic snick. Alexis froze, watched the door open, saw a slender, shadowy figure slip inside. The silhouette was barely visible, black against blacker. A slender person, not short and stocky like Mel. Alexis lay completely still and breathed evenly, as if she were asleep. A ball of anxiety formed in her belly, as she awaited the worst.

Alexis could sense a person approaching, stealthy as a tiger. Squinting, she could make out this person's silhouette beside her.

She wondered how fast Mel would respond if she screamed.

Then, a hand was laid, light as a feather on her head. The hand made slow sweeping strokes over her hair, giving her goosebumps. *I know the feel of that hand! That clean smell.*

The hand slowed but didn't leave her hair. "Alexis. I'm sorry," a man said.

That voice. Alexis sat bolt upright. *It can't be.*

"Turn on the light," she said, her voice choked with emotion.

The man walked over to the light switch and flipped it on to reveal the last person she ever expected to see.

140

For a moment, Alexis didn't know whether to scream, cry her eyes out, or simply run over and hug him as hard as she could. And in that moment--an eternity, really--she simply gaped at him, unable to speak.

Finally, she got her bearings. Half convinced she was seeing a ghost, she uttered his name.

"Daniel?"

CHAPTER THIRTY-TWO

JESSICA

I stopped reading, leaned back in my chair, and sighed. If I couldn't sleep, I was going to put all my nervous energy to good use.

Unfortunately, this exercise had provided no ready answers to my situation. I rose and checked the drawers of a nightstand, where I found a pen and a hotel pad. Scribbling a note, I tore the page off, folded it, and tucked it in my jeans pocket. Doodling did nothing to relieve the stress. My obligations threatened to overwhelm me.

I squeezed my eyes shut and tried to tune out my thoughts. *Focus on something else.* Exhausted, I slouched in the chair, elbows perched on the armrests. I closed my eyes and tried to clear my mind.

I must have drifted off because I was transported back to the university campus in Boulder. Fred and I were walking toward a large brick building, fronted with a line of trees. We were speaking of inconsequential things. Fred was smiling. As we approached the big brick building, a man emerged and moved toward us. As he grew closer, I recognized Selby. He waved and came up to talk to Fred. The building. What was it? It had a name. It was . . . .

I jerked awake. Early morning light leaked through the blinds. I blinked several times, trying to think.

"Ah . . . ." It was all I could manage to get out. Right on the tip of my tongue. Damn! What was the name?

A rap at the door, then Liz's voice. "Are you up, Jess?"

"Yeah, yeah," I assured her. "Give me just a minute."

I snapped my fingers, as if the action could conjure up memories. "I know it. I know the place. What the hell is it?"

A big brick building. And Selby was a scientist. It started with a P. No, no, not a P.

Feeling frustrated, I tried not to think about it. It was the kind of information that would have to come to me in its own good time.

I took a quick shower, pulled on my clothes, and stumbled downstairs, drawn by the rich, intoxicating aroma of coffee and the unmistakable sizzle of bacon on a grill. Imagine my dismay when I saw I'd be sharing my breakfast with George Clooney and his twin sister.

I wandered into the breakfast nook where the twins sat at a table. George had just shoveled a forkful of eggs in his mouth when he saw me. His eyes lit up briefly in recognition, but quickly faded when I didn't return the enthusiasm.

"Good morning," he ventured.

"Yeah, hi." I nodded to George and his twin (whose name remained a mystery). Pulling out a chair, I sank into it and went into what was becoming a most familiar posture—holding my head in my hands.

"Are you okay?" I heard Liz ask from the kitchen, where I caught a glimpse of her working the pans on the stove with the speed of the Iron Chef.

"I couldn't sleep a wink." I yawned and rubbed my face to accentuate the foggy mental conditions I was working under.

"I'll have eggs and bacon ready in a second."

"Coffee." I dredged the word up and it hung in the air, like an unanswered question. I started to push myself up to retrieve a cup, only to feel a hand on my shoulder.

George was by my side with a steaming mug of the brew. He set it on the table before me. "Voila."

For a moment, I was at a loss for words, looking into those gentle brown eyes. Finally, foggy mind and all, I remembered my manners and said, "Thank you." *Who would have thought I'd be thanking this man for anything?*

As we ate, George went over the plan. They'd take me back to Liz's. After that, it was a simple matter of having their operative "drop the dime" on me, so to speak. By doing this, the operative should gain more of the group's respect and trust. And my capture could be made "swift and painless," as George had mentioned before.

After that, I needed to dig for whatever information I could. "Focus on Selby's role. Obviously, it was important. We need to know exactly what he was doing for them."

"If Selby was so important, then why did they kill Fred?" I asked. I was so fatigued, I thought I might be missing something.

"We think Fred might have stumbled across something bigger." George said. "He may have been doing research for your book but could have found out about other, bigger things."

I nodded and exhaled a shuddering sigh. "Great. I'm responsible for Fred's death. That's just what I need first thing in the morning."

George must have heard the despair in my voice. He leaned toward me. In a calm and deliberate tone, he said, "He chose to do what he did. He may have done it for you, but you didn't force him."

I shrugged my acquiescence. *Sure. That's what I'll tell myself.*

"How do you know Selby's the key?"

George started to speak, but nothing came out. "Sorry. Need to . . . ."

"Yes, I get it!" I snapped. "Need to know only. Gee, where have I heard that before?"

George stared at me, eyes intent with something approaching fear. My arms and neck broke out in gooseflesh.

"Believe me," he murmured. "You're better off *not* knowing the possibilities."

I inhaled sharply, suddenly aware that I'd been holding my breath.

"Shouldn't I at least know who your operative is?" I asked. "So I can contact him."

"The operative will contact you," George said. His look told me this was a non-negotiable point. "You can pool your notes and get a sense of what these folks are really up to."

"Do you think they'll get suspicious and check me for a wire?" I asked.

"Ah." George held up a finger. "You're wearing jeans. This should fit."

He produced a leather belt that was something less than Gucci, but could pass for high quality.

"There's a tracking device and transmitter here." He showed me the unremarkable gray rectangle hidden behind the buckle. "All you do is pretend to adjust your belt and hit this tiny micro-switch." He pointed at a small protuberance in the metal. "Want to practice?"

I spent the next ten minutes, repeatedly adjusting the belt in a way that would hopefully look innocuous. The first couple of times seemed awkward, but with repetition, the move became easier.

Meanwhile, George tested out the receiver from upstairs. "Loud and clear!" he announced, each time we ran the test.

"Okay," he said, upon his return. He looked almost proud of me. "You're good. You'll be fine."

"I guess I'd make a pretty good spy, huh?"

George drew close and gave me a mock conspiratorial look. "They're called agents, Mrs. Lambert." He smiled to underscore the joke.

I knew the line. Walter Matthau said it in *Charade*, a movie about a widow who blunders into a situation involving stolen money and a pack of rogues who are convinced she has it. Matthau played a fake U.S. intelligence agent who claims he needs her help.

For the first time in I don't know how long, I laughed.

CHAPTER THIRTY-THREE

JESSICA

The plan was for me to return to Liz's apartment by cab. As George and his nameless twin busied themselves preparing to leave, Liz drew me aside, out of their earshot.

"Don't worry. I have your back, too," she murmured.

"What do you mean?" I whispered, checking my belt buckle reflexively to make sure I hadn't left the hidden listening device on.

"I'll keep the security detail in the wings. Just in case."

Just in case what? From what I'd seen of Cotter and his sidekick Billy, I wasn't overly impressed. Cotter seemed capable enough, but Billy? I sincerely hoped the Feds would come through in an emergency, because I didn't want to rely on the Abbott and Costello of security guard teams.

"Could you do me favor?" I asked Liz, digging the note from my pocket. "If anything happens to me, please give this to Mom and Dad."

Liz opened her mouth but shut it fast.

"Just put it in an envelope and mail it," I said. "I know you and they . . . haven't been close. But please . . . do this for me."

Liz nodded and took the note.

Once I'd settled back into Liz's condo, the next step was for me to go out in public. I grabbed my laptop, which a government agent had recovered from the hotel and obligingly delivered, and headed out to the nearest coffee shop. I found my way to Pennsylvania Avenue—D.C.'s version of Main Street as laid out by Pierre Charles L'Enfant. I thought of L'Enfant as I wandered into a coffee shop called Le Pain Quotidien.

I grabbed a large coffee and a chocolate croissant. It was the least I could do for myself if I was going to be kidnapped.

I took a table facing the big picture window. Peering out to the street, I saw no sign of my dynamic bodyguard duo. None that was obvious, anyway.

I set up the laptop and opened the file I'd been working on in the wee hours. Did I want to continue the story or revise what I'd written? I'd been so busy thinking about my imminent capture that worrying about Alexis' situation seemed almost ridiculous.

Use it. The words floated through my mind. I *was* in her situation. (Well, except for her dead fiancé showing up, of course.) Who would understand better how she would react? *So use it.* Tuning out the chatter of customers around me, I plunged into reviewing the latest draft.

φφφ

ALEXIS

Daniel gazed back at me, a weak smile on his lips and an apology in his eyes. "I'm sorry."

"Sorry?" Alexis jumped out of bed and ran over to him, wrapping him in a hug that would make a python proud. She sobbed on his shoulder, heaving with relief and confusion.

"I'm sorry I couldn't tell you." Daniel's voice was choked, either from emotion or Alexis' astonishing grip on him.

Alexis let go, stepped back and looked at him. "All this time. All this time." She shook her head, unable to go on.

Once disengaged from her hug, Daniel took a deep breath. "They made me promise, Alexis."

"Who? The NSA?"

He shook his head. "These guys were with Homeland Security."

"Jesus." *How many agencies were involved?*

Daniel drew Alexis to him once again, enveloping her in his arms. "God, how I wanted to tell you. After my accident, I woke up in a hospital bed. They had a guard outside my door, and a man came by to question me."

Daniel pulled back and looked into Alexis's eyes. "He told me his name was Benson. Agent Benson showed me a badge and identification. Apparently, he'd been tailing me the night of the crash. Swede and I had both been under surveillance. I didn't believe him at first. I might even have ignored him, if I hadn't noticed he was carrying a gun."

He paused a moment, looking distracted, as if he might have forgotten to turn the stove off. Alexis knew that look. It was a habit that had once annoyed her, but now she ate it up with a spoon.

"After the hospital released me, Benson took me to the federal building in Portland," he continued. "I was in a room full of people from a whole alphabet soup of agencies. They'd known about the research Swede and I had been doing for a while.

"But they'd always kept their distance. So the people who first contacted us weren't with them. Apparently, we were right to be suspicious."

Alexis struggled to take this in from a man she thought had been dead. "So, those people who

approached you before that . . . *they* were
terrorists?"

"I guess so. That's what the Feds say anyhow."

"And how do we know these guys are the good guys?"

Daniel threw up his hands. "Unless the terrorists
have reserved a room in a federal building, I think
it's safe to assume we're dealing with the real
thing."

Alexis started to question what secret agenda the
federal authorities might have and then thought
better of it. *Whatever their interest, it beats
terrorism, right?*

"Two questions," she said. "What on earth were you
guys working on? And don't be evasive. I have a right
to know."

Daniel heaved a sigh. "Okay. Einstein's theory is
what we call a gauge theory--everything is described
with reference to the speed of light, which is a
universal constant that forms a framework for the
theory. Magueijo's approach removes the speed of
light as a constant by making it variable, by making
it less of a determinate certainty; and this produces
a theory without a stable backdrop--a theory in which
events define what space is like, instead of space
determining what events happen within it. So our
research is about bringing the variability or
uncertainty of quantum mechanics into the all-
encompassing and relative universe. Or you could say
it's about introducing the curvatures of relative
space-time into the atomically flat dimensions of
quantum mechanics."

Alexis shook her head and waved her hands. "Stop,
stop, stop. In English, please. The Physics for
Dummies version."

Daniel grinned. "Here's the bottom line. This was
never about building bigger bombs. Once the hydrogen

bomb was invented, there was no limit to the size a hydrogen bomb could be. They can always be made bigger by using more material to feed the fusion reaction.

"My research proved we could create an entirely different kind of weapon--a quantum gravity weapon. Fusing together Planck particles would be akin to smashing tiny black holes together and generating pulses of gravity waves. But we don't know what immediate effects those waves would have in close proximity.

"So, we're not talking about creating a greater explosion. We're talking about a concentrated waveform that changes the way matter *exists* in space. This could be a wavefront that causes chemical bonds to break and everyday objects to collapse at a molecular level into dust, vapor, and flame. Or it could cause an uncontrollable nuclear reaction releasing unimaginable amounts of energy, consuming everything as surely as if uranium or plutonium atoms were all that were involved."

Lips parted, Alexis looked frozen. "Sounds like Armageddon," she whispered. Her expression transformed from one of horror to a scowl. "Why didn't they tell me you were alive?"

Daniel gave a wan smile. "They wanted everyone to think I was dead, so the terrorists would focus on Swede. Following only one person made their investigation easier, less labor-intensive."

"So," Alexis said. "I assume that what Mel and I are going to discuss tomorrow is how to get me back to my sister's, get your research, and take it to the Feds."

Daniel nodded, looking sheepish. "Yeah. That's it."

"Basically, I have to pretend I don't know who
these people really are and convince my sister to
tell me where your research is hidden?"

"Yes."

Alexis blew out a breath. "I wish I'd taken acting
lessons."

"And I wish I could do it instead." Daniel grabbed
her arms and gazed at her, his eyes drinking her in
like a life-sustaining glass of water on a hot day.
"But I need to stay dead. At least, until this is
over."

Alexis felt tears welling in her eyes again. "I
wish to hell it were over now."

φφφ

JESSICA

I took a quick break from reading. My plan all along had been to
bring Daniel "back from the dead," but I wondered if doing so
at this point was more a function of good plotting or simply
wishing Fred could be brought back, too. As I thought this over,
a spark of recognition went off in my mind. What was it? The
agent's name. The one Daniel mentioned.

"Benson," I said aloud. The woman at the next table shot me
a look, then glued her eyes back on her iPhone.

I mouthed the word silently, which must have looked odd.
Benson . . . Benson . . . . Then, I remembered the dream. Fred and
Selby. The building Selby had emerged from. It had a name.

"Benson Earth Sciences Building. Holy shit." I blurted the
words loud enough that the woman with the iPhone got up and
moved to another table.

Now I remembered. Selby was a geologist. Then, I
remembered his specialty. Plate tectonics.

Earthquakes, caused by the movement of the earth's plates
against one another. And San Francisco was located right on the

San Andreas Fault, where two major plates ground against each other. I imagined a nightmare scenario in which terrorists might try to trigger a major quake—or more than one. Fault lines like the San Andreas could be found all over the planet. If the group caused enough earthquakes, millions (or even billions) could die. And my parents were close to ground zero.

CHAPTER THIRTY-FOUR

JESSICA

For a moment, this revelation stunned me to the point where I simply sat and stared through the picture window fronting the store. People walked by, moving in and out of view at random intervals. They barely registered on my mental radar. People going about their business, not imagining the horror I envisioned.

Could that really be the truth? Or am I just letting my imagination run away from me?

Someone touched my shoulder and I started with a grunt. My heart was beating its way out of my rib cage. I gulped air as if I'd been drowning.

"Are you all right, Miss?"

I gazed up into the milk chocolate face of a motherly looking woman with honey golden eyes beneath a furrowed brow.

"Are you feeling okay?" she asked.

I realized I was staring and stuttered, "I'm . . . I'm fine, really. Just have a lot on my mind today."

"Uh huh." The woman neither looked nor sounded convinced. Her brow relaxed, but she still looked doubtful.

"I'm okay. Honest." I even managed a smile. Hopefully, a convincing one.

"Well, girl, you turned pale as a ghost. I thought you were going to pass out."

Well, that's only because I know that a bunch of extremists are going to kill millions and millions of people. And I need to figure out how to stop them before they do it. No biggie, right?

The look of concern returned to the woman's face. I realized I'd been staring again.

"I'm okay now," I blurted. "I . . . I didn't get much sleep last night. I'm really tired." This last sentence was spoken with the conviction of one who's weary to the bone of everything, as I certainly was.

The woman looked a bit more—if not completely—reassured by these words. "All right, honey. You shouldn't push yourself too hard. Bad for your health."

This seemed to open the door to any number of rejoinders. But I simply said, "I'll keep that in mind. Thanks."

I tried to push the horrible thought aside. I had no proof of the group's plans, but what other part would a geologist play? I reviewed more of the story—a scene about the morning after, Mel briefing Alexis about what she needed to do (having just been through the drill, it was almost like writing in a diary). Not a thing here about geology, but how Swede and Daniel had debunked Magueijo's footnote about the benign nature of his theory and had research to support the nightmare scenario that a weapon even more destructive than the atom bomb could be created.

"Jeez!" I said, exhausted from lack of sleep and agonizing over the story (not to mention my impending "kidnapping"). "Enough." I saved my files again and shut down the laptop.

As I packed my equipment into my carrier, I noticed a car slow as it moved past the store. I thought it might be looking for a parking spot, but it passed a perfectly good one.

The car was bland and indistinguishable. A late model compact, grayish-blue.

I watched it turn the corner, out of sight.

Hmm. I wonder if that's my ride.

I slung my purse over my shoulder, grabbed the carrying case, and tossed my trash on the way out.

I headed back to Liz's place. It was mid-afternoon, almost 2:00 according to my cell phone. Even so, the streets were full of people. Purposeful men and women in suits, talking up a storm into their phones. Many of them with Bluetooth phones plugged into their ears seemed to be babbling to the air.

"Man," I muttered. "I used to be able to tell who was crazy." I smiled and shook my head at how this sentence so aptly summed up my life now.

My stroll back to Liz's took me past a narrow alley. As I stepped onto the corner and prepared to cross, I saw the grayish-blue compact parked beside the building. I heard the door open but kept walking. I felt her presence before she pressed a gun into my back.

"Hi. Great to see you," Cynthia said. She hooked her arm through mine and steered me toward the car.

I breathed a sigh. Well, it was better than getting bashed over the head.

CHAPTER THIRTY-FIVE

JOE

Billy returned with coffee and sandwiches for the two of them. Cotter took his cup and sipped the hot brew.

"They've moved to the alley," he told Billy. He'd first spotted the bluish-gray compact because of its severely dented rear fender. He could have sworn he'd seen a similar vehicle with that distinguishing mark at the Navy Memorial. The car had been parked down the street from the coffee shop for hours. It pulled out and rolled past the shop, then hung a right. From where they sat half a block away from the alley's entrance, Cotter could make out at least three people in the car.

Jessica left the coffee shop and proceeded toward them. Cotter jolted to alert.

He saw Jessica stop and look to her right. Then she moved into the alley, out of view.

"It's on," he said, starting the car.

Billy grinned. "All right!"

Cotter shot him an exasperated look. Could this kid possibly be as naïve as he seemed? Cotter shook his head, then checked traffic before pulling away from the curb and moving toward the alley. He edged into the intersection, looked for the car, and caught the sight of the compact's taillights glowing in the shadows.

Cotter swung a hard left to follow—at a distance.

Billy's phone rang. He checked the caller ID. "It's just my Mom."

"Okay, whatever." Cotter focused on the car ahead and tried not to get too close.

Billy answered. "Hey, Mom . . . . Yeah . . . . We're fine . . . . Mom, I gotta go, okay? See you later."

As Billy closed the phone, Cotter glanced over. The hint of a smile played on the young man's lips.

At the alley's end, the bluish car turned right. Cotter hurried to catch up. He reached the intersection, looked right, and saw the car stopped at a red light.

Cotter used the moment to snatch Billy's phone from his hands. As Billy sputtered, Cotter checked the last call received. A private number.

"Billy, how did you know it was your moth—?" Cotter's question was cut off by a right uppercut to the chin.

CHAPTER THIRTY-SIX

JESSICA

"So nice to see you again, Cyn," I said. "While I could see you, that is."

Once bundled into the car, I was blindfolded. Apparently, I wasn't even going to get a cheap tour of D.C. out of this ride to . . . wherever.

"Relax," Cyn said, her voice dripping with venom.

"Kind of hard to do that blindfolded. And with no idea where you're taking me. Or what you want from me."

"I see you have your laptop." Cynthia snickered. "You and that story of yours." Her voice was filled with disbelief.

"Maybe I can help you," I said. "I . . . I want to cooperate if I can. I'm . . . just not sure I know how." At this point, I knew the agents were listening in. I'd managed to hit the switch on my buckle while pretending to adjust my seatbelt.

Cynthia fell quiet. The only sound was that of road noises and traffic.

"Can you be more specific about what you *need* from me?" My voice tweaked up a notch. I hoped I wasn't overplaying my hand. That is, assuming I could even guess what game we were playing.

"Why don't you just sit back, relax, and enjoy the ride," Cynthia said. "We'll get into specifics when we get there."

Can't wait. After trying to count turns and listen for clues, I finally gave up and took her advice. The only sound in the car was the road's hum beneath the tires.

After what seemed like hours, we arrived. My door opened and someone grabbed my arm.

"Let's go." A man spoke the two words as if he were hard-pressed to share them.

He pulled me from the car and maneuvered me across what felt like grass. I tried to keep my wits and my balance. The only sounds were birds and distant traffic. We could be in a quiet suburb or in the middle of nowhere.

My feet hit pavement. A path? We halted. Keys jingled and a lock turned. I heard a door open and was then guided up one step and inside.

Two people, each holding my arms, led me further inside. My tennis shoes squeaked on the hardwood floor.

They lowered me into a chair. My face felt warm and I sensed a light shining beyond the blindfold.

Someone tore the blindfold off and I blinked into the brightness. A light was directed at my face. Eventually, I made out a windowless room, barely furnished with a couple of chairs, a cot, and a desk with a shelf holding a fax or printer.

A heavy-set man with a swarthy complexion squatted beside me. I gripped my carrying case in front of me, like a shield. My purse still hung from my shoulder.

"Now," the man said. "Tell us what you know."

"A-about what?" I managed to stammer. My mouth felt dry and pasty.

"About our plans. What did they tell you?"

I tried to think about how I'd been instructed to play this, but my memory failed me. I'd just have to play it by ear.

"Nothing. I don't know about any plans."

"How do you know Selby?"

I opened my mouth, but realized it was a trick question. This man wanted me to admit I knew Selby, but I didn't really.

"Who?"

"That guy who was talking to you at the Navy Memorial. What did he say?"

"Oh, him. Jeez! Thanks to you, he keeled over before he could say anything."

The man rose and moved around me, inspecting me from all angles.

"What makes you think we did that?" His voice taunted me.

Who else? I wanted to say.

"We know you've met Selby before," the man said, sounding impatient.

I froze. *How long have these people been watching me?*

"Your friend, Fred, introduced you. Am I right?"

Stunned, I nodded.

"What do you know about Selby? Anything at all?"

I had to say something here to appease the man.

"I . . . I know he's a geologist."

The man squatted beside me again and grabbed my arm. *Wrong answer.* I felt panic pour through me. "Are you sure that's all you know?" the man said, his voice raspy, his eyes probing me like X-rays.

"It's no use, Lucius." Cynthia spoke up.

Lucius gave her a blank look, then rose to his full height, leaving me staring at his crotch. "I think he needs to talk to her." Lucius emphasized the word "he" as if the "h" should be capitalized.

Lucius ambled out the door. Cynthia and I said nothing. My eyes searched her out, but she averted her gaze.

A tall dark-haired man in his forties, rangy with leathery tan skin, entered and strode up to me. I assumed this must be the "he" that Lucius referred to—probably their leader. His eyes were smoldering, black coals with a look of some internal madness or obsession embedded in a hard, pitted face. He began pacing, keeping his eyes on me. "What will we do with you, young lady?"

He seemed amused.

"Just don't hurt me, please," I said, my lines coming back to me. "I don't know what you're up to, but believe me, I'm not your enemy."

The man stopped and peered at me.

"Honest." I gulped. "The Feds are after me, but I don't want any part of it. They think I'm on their side, but I'm not. I'm just a writer. I'm on no one's side but my own."

Cynthia started to say something, but the dark-haired man held up a hand to silence her.

"Why are you pretending to help the Feds?" he asked.

"I told you. They've been after me, and I'm just playing along, so they'll leave me alone."

"I'm not sure I believe you."

"Why would I lie?" As I said it, I thought of several reasons.

He leaned toward me. "You tell me," he said, as if he'd read my mind.

I merely shook my head. "I'm not lying. I swear it." I felt like I was vying for an Academy Award against Meryl Streep.

The man straightened and turned to Cynthia, who leaned against the desk.

"Let's give her some time to think about it," he said. He turned to me and added, "I want you to write down anything Fred or Selby told you. Anything. It's important." He turned on his heel and stalked out.

Cynthia looked at me and rapped her knuckles softly on the desk. She walked over to the lamp and shut it off.

"You can use your laptop at the desk or write it by hand." Cynthia jerked her head a couple of times toward the desk. She stared at me intently, as if trying to send a telepathic message.

I realized she wasn't pointing a gun at me anymore. I rose.

"Careful," she said. "Don't be stupid."

"No. No, I'll cooperate." My tongue felt like it was coated with glue. "Could I have some water? I think I'm entitled, as a . . . what? . . . prisoner?"

She nodded. "No problem. I'll take care of that. Meanwhile, you need to get to work."

For a moment, I relaxed and drew a deep breath. Cyn moved to the desk, picked up a pad and pen, and turned to me. "They're listening," she mouthed, as she handed me the writing implements and then left the room.

I pondered Cyn's behavior. *What now?* Gathering my wits, I trudged over to the desk, placed my laptop on it and sat down. What could I tell them that wouldn't get me in trouble? All I had were suppositions based on what little I knew.

I pulled out the laptop and set it up. Turning it on, I tried to think of anything Fred or Selby had actually said about the group and came up empty. Well, that wouldn't take long to write.

All I knew was that Fred had joined the group to help me research my novel about terrorists who were exploring the darker repercussions of a new physics theory that challenged Einstein's relativity model.

I knew Selby studied geology, including plate tectonics.

I had no idea what one had to do with the other, if anything. All I had were assumptions about fault lines and earthquakes.

I was typing out these pitiful bits of information, when Cyn walked in with bottled water.

"Please excuse the informality," she said, handing me the bottle. I twisted the cap and lifted it to my lips, knocking back almost half the contents.

After pausing for breath, I swiped my hand over my mouth. "Thanks. I was parched."

"Take all the time you need." Cyn pulled a drawer open and, without a word, pointed inside. It held a small black rectangle. I picked it up and examined it. It had a USB port at one end. A flash drive.

This can't be an accident. I thought of Cynthia, cocking her head toward the desk.

My eyes narrowed. *What was Cyn up to?*

CHAPTER THIRTY-SEVEN

JESSICA

I glanced about, wondering about hidden cameras or microphones, then positioned the flash drive at the USB port and paused to consider before I shoved it into place.

I accessed the flash drive and found several folders. I opened one that said "Invoices." This displayed an array of files. Word and PDF documents.

At random, I double-clicked a file. It was an invoice for drilling equipment. I shook my head and tried opening another. Geologic surveys.

"What the . . . .?" I shut my mouth. If the room was bugged, I didn't want to clue anyone in on my thoughts. Were these people drilling around fault lines? Planting explosives? Mining uranium? Is that what Selby's part in all this was?

I shook my head at that last thought. *Not uranium. They could probably pick up the materials to make a bomb on the black market much more easily than they could dig for it themselves.*

I went back to the folders and found one that read "Maps." I opened it to see even more files—all PDFs.

I clicked on one and saw a topographical map. Could it be of the San Andreas Fault? It didn't look like it. I saw a river, but that was all. I was still straining to find a fault line when Lucius came inside.

Before I could act, Lucius strode over. "What are you doing?" Cyn stood to my other side, saying nothing.

He stood beside me, glaring at the computer screen.

Lucius' face turned red, then purple with rage. He started to speak, but all I heard was an odd popping sound. Open-mouthed, Lucius stumbled and grabbed the desk. He'd sprung a leak in his upper chest and blood spurted out.

I heard the noise again and Lucius collapsed. I looked at Cyn, who held a silenced pistol, still smoldering from the shots. I started to say something, but she lifted a finger to her lips and moved toward me. With shaky hands, I switched back to the document I'd been working on and typed, "WTF?"

"It looks like you're making progress," she said aloud, setting the gun on the desk and placing her hands on the keyboard.

She typed, "Room is bugged. Copied files from their computer this AM. Haven't seen yet."

I considered how to proceed. *How do I word this? Is this a trap?* Finally, I typed, "Why?"

Cyn read my response and typed, "I'm undercover with Feds. Do files make sense?"

I blinked and stared. *All this time.* Who would've known Cynthia was the operative?

CHAPTER THIRTY-EIGHT

JESSICA

I realized I should respond to Cynthia's remark. "I'm remembering a few things. Not much," I stated for the record. I typed, "Need to talk," and hammered my finger down on the period key.

Cyn nodded. "Do the best you can. That's all we can ask," she said for the benefit of unseen listeners.

She took over at the keyboard and typed, "Hard to arrange. Shooting Lucius wasn't part of the plan, but I'll come up with an excuse. You understand I needed to make it look like I hated you?" Cyn continued to type, but I knew where she was going. That explained her behavior at the hotel. Why she slapped me so hard. She had to regain whatever trust she'd built with this group of wackos. She'd only just managed to get hold of the data, but hadn't seen it yet. And she wasn't sure how to get it into the right hands without implicating herself.

Cyn was still typing, when I grabbed the pencil. "Why didn't the Feds just TELL me about you?" I scribbled.

Cyn looked abashed. She typed, "Probably didn't want you to accidentally give me away. You might have betrayed me with a tell."

I gave her a thumbs up. *Damn that George, anyway. Did he think I was an idiot?* I had to admit, though, it was a smart move on his part.

"I'm writing everything I can remember," I said, to keep the dialogue going. I took over at the keyboard. "Selby was a geologist who studied tectonics," I typed. "Does that help?"

"Good," Cyn said, adopting a tough tone. "Get it all down in detail." As she spoke, Cyn brought up the map on the screen and squinted at it. She frowned. Her jaw dropped and her eyebrows shot up. She switched back to the word processing program and typed, "Did he study geophysics?"

I looked at the sentence. I had no idea. I couldn't tell you the difference between the two. I shrugged, feeling helpless.

Cyn continued typing. This was putting on a good show for the hidden microphone, anyway. She stopped and I read, "Have you heard the news about the earthquake activity in Yellowstone?"

Yellowstone? I shook my head. *What about the Golden Gate Bridge?*

Cyn typed at length. When she stopped, I read what was on the screen.

She'd written, "This could be worse than we imagined, if Selby's job is what I think. Our theory was that the group might blow up a major landmark. But these maps are cause for even greater concern. We're talking about a catastrophe that could wipe out the entire continent, maybe half the planet."

There it was again. The threat of near annihilation. I looked at Cyn, no doubt conveying disbelief. "How???" I mouthed.

Cyn paused, exhaled, and typed another note. It read, "By causing the supervolcano in Yellowstone to erupt."

CHAPTER THIRTY-NINE

JESSICA

I stared at Cyn's statement, unable to form a coherent response.
Finally, I typed: *What are you talking about???*

"Can you work any faster?" Cyn said, aloud.

"I'm trying, okay?"

Cyn took over the keyboard and pounded out a reply, as I
tried to make sense of the situation. I'd never been to
Yellowstone, but I knew it was the site of Old Faithful, the
geyser that shot off with amazing regularity. Along with being an
awesome and popular nature preserve, the park was the site of
many hot water springs and geysers. So, what causes hot water
springs? Clearly, there must be a heat source within the earth.
That heat source would have to be intense. Hot enough to
create molten lava. Then I said to myself, *Consider Yellowstone's
location.* Not far from the Pacific Rim and the volcanic
mountains in the Cascades. Mountains like Mt. Hood, Mt.
Adams, Mt. Rainier and, of course, the infamous Mount St.
Helen's. But I had no idea that Yellowstone itself was part of a
volcano.

I read along as Cyn typed her missive:

Homeland Sec's been watching Yellowstone Park a while. Park is located within basin—crater of one of earth's biggest volcanoes. Thought to be extinct. But it's active and geologists watching with concern. Recently, ground's been swelling and there's been more earthquakes. According to scientists, this could mean Yellowstone coming close to eruption.

I read this with alarm and typed: *So the drilling could be to plant explosives to push it past the brink?*

Cyn nodded.

"Jesus," I whispered. The word slipped through my lips, like an exhalation.

I typed: *What are the chances this will work? Wouldn't they need massive explosives?*

Cyn's response: *We think they've been stockpiling nuclear weaponry. Easy to do these days. Terrorists network on the Internet. It's beyond frightening what they can get. Bombs in the right places could cause the biggest explosion in centuries. Since the last time Yellowstone erupted.*

I cringed at her response. *What happened last time?* I typed.

Cyn wrote: *Ash spread for thousands of miles. Boulders blew halfway across the continent. Explosion spewed enough debris to fill Grand Canyon. Destroyed almost the entire western half of North America. But winds carried ash around the world, disrupting our eco-systems. This could kill millions, even billions, and affect everyone. Global economy would collapse. And imagine the hospitals and emergency service systems. People would die or panic.*

I digested this information. *If their plan works, of course,* I wrote.

Cyn typed: *That's a big 'if.' Do you want to take a chance that it won't?*

CHAPTER FORTY

JESSICA

Cynthia mouthed the words, "Keep typing." She seemed to be pondering as I did. "What happens now?" I wrote.

Cyn snapped to attention. "Finished?" She nodded to show I should answer in the affirmative.

"Yeah. I'm done," I announced.

"Good," she said. "Let's take a look."

I wondered why the public hadn't been warned but had a feeling I already knew. Such information would likely cause folks to panic. Homeland Security would want to nip this in the bud before the group had a chance to make it happen. They'd want to keep the matter quiet for any number of reasons. All the businesses and local economies would be affected by a rash announcement of an impending supervolcano explosion. Besides, it was preventable, if we could just get the information to the right people in time.

"This will do," Cyn said. "You can pack up now." She hooked the laptop to the device on the shelf, printed our typed Q and A, saved it to a thumb drive, and then deleted it from my laptop. I removed Cynthia's flash drive, stowed it with the thumb drive in my purse, and shut the laptop down. After I packed the computer and printout, she handed me her gun. I stared at it, unwilling to move or handle it. *What am I supposed to do with this?*

Cyn pulled out a notepad and pencil: *Hit me on the head with the gun. Hard as you can. When I fall, run. Turn right, go down the hall, look for door. Notify Feds. They'll pick you up.*

I shook my head. She mouthed, "Do it."

I gawked at the gun. Then at her face. I couldn't.

"Do it," she mouthed again. Cyn looked impatient.

I realized this was supposed to be my escape. I knew what I had to do.

"I'm sorry," I mouthed as I hauled back and swung the gun at her.

Cyn winced, but she took the hit like a pro. I felt sick.

I looped the strap of my laptop case across the opposite shoulder, my purse across the other.

Still wincing, Cyn stared at me with raised eyebrows that asked, "Ready?"

I wasn't but I didn't have a choice.

Cyn upended the chair. She let herself slump to the floor. I ran.

CHAPTER FORTY-ONE

JESSICA

I made a break for the front door, expecting to see the crazy-eyed man or one of his cohorts, but apparently they'd left me in Cynthia's and Lucius' capable hands. This seemed almost too easy.

As I reached for the doorknob, a large pair of men's hands grabbed my arms from behind. I kicked and thrashed until I got an arm free and went for his eyes. But he caught my hand and pulled me close until I couldn't move at all.

I remembered the listening device and screamed.

The man's grip didn't loosen. "Jesus, lady. You trying to make me deaf?"

I stood there, stupidly, waiting for the rescue team.

Someone knocked at the door. We eyed each other. *Who'd be knocking? Jehovah's Witnesses?*

My captor moved around me, careful to keep a tight grip with one arm around my waist. A bald edifice of flesh, he checked the peephole. "No one's there," he said.

He turned toward me and was about to speak when the front window shattered. We both hit the floor.

"What the . . . ? The man rolled off me, displayed a holstered gun, and muttered, "Don't move." He peered into the living room, got up, and retrieved a brick from the floor.

He glared at me. I shook my head. Clearly, it wasn't from the rescue team.

"Hmmph." The bald man rose, unholstered the handgun and strode to the door, opening it. He surveyed the yard. I followed suit and peered out from behind him.

"I dunno." He shrugged and started to close the door. A pistol appeared at his temple.

My gaze moved up the arm with the pistol to find Billy.

CHAPTER FORTY-TWO

JESSICA

Billy was smiling, although he didn't look quite like himself. His eyes had an odd glow. As if he were relishing the moment.

The bald man tried turning his head toward the gun. Billy yelled, "Don't move, motherfucker! I'll blow your brains out."

All I could think to say was, "Thank God you're here. What took so long? Where's your partner?"

"He got delayed. Never mind him." Billy seemed lit with an internal fire.

The bald man, who stood frozen to the spot, ventured a thought. "Look, son. Put the weapon down. Let's talk about this."

Billy only jammed the gun harder against the man's temple.

"Are you really ready to shoot a man in cold blood?" the bald man asked.

Billy smile widened. A shot roared and echoed through the room.

Bloody grayish brain matter splattered all over me, the doorframe, and the wall. The debris speckled Billy's clothing, too. The bald man had crumpled to the floor, his skull half blown away.

I did a dry heave, then another.
Billy lowered his weapon. "I was born ready."

CHAPTER FORTY-THREE

JESSICA

"Why?" I sputtered, struggling not to lose the croissant and coffee I'd had earlier.

"Because I could." The words seemed to come from another being. Not Billy. *Was he possessed? Brainwashed?*

I was still trying to make sense of the situation, when he grabbed my arm. "Let's get out of here."

I didn't resist.

He ran, me stumbling beside him, to where he'd parked a mid-sized car behind a hedge. I tried to think. How could I delay our departure?

"Wait," he said. "Take off the belt."

"What?"

He pointed the gun at me. "You heard me. Take it off."

Oh, shit. Where was the goddamned rescue team?

Billy glared at me. "Do it. Now."

CHAPTER FORTY-FOUR

JOE

When Cotter woke up, his first view was of a brick wall. He tried to move and invisible blades stabbed his skull and lower back.

Cotter groaned with the effort of trying to stretch his arms. His head throbbed in time with his heartbeat. Lying still in an attempt to ease the pain, his nostrils flared at the stench of urine and body odor.

What the hell . . . ?

He and Billy had been following the car that had taken Jessica. They had stopped at the end of an alley, where he was now sprawled like a drunk. People didn't notice bums lying in alleys in D.C. If anything, they went out of their way to avoid them.

"Billy?" he croaked. *Damn you.*

After a time, Cotter fumbled for his cell phone. Missing. Of course. He eased to his feet and staggered from the alley, seeking a pay phone. There had to be one left somewhere on the planet.

The street was mixed residential and retail. A few restaurants, a used bookstore, a vintage clothing store. He spotted a phone

booth and stumbled toward it, only to find the receiver torn
from the apparatus.

"Shit, who uses pay phones?" He saw a passing man in a suit.
"Excuse me, sir. Could I use your phone?"

The man looked at him askance a moment and quickened his
pace, staring straight ahead.

"Excuse me!" He tried again with a couple. They shook their
heads in unison. "I'm sorry," the man said, though he didn't
sound sorry. They hurried away.

Cotter stopped to consider how he must look. He realized
his shirt was wrinkled and dirty, his pants crusted with filth.
He'd been lying in an alley for . . . God knows how long. He
checked for his watch. *Thank God, I still have that.* Almost two
hours had passed.

He tested his cheek, which was tender, along with the knot
at the back of his skull. He glanced at his reflection in the
window of a parked car. His face was bruised and dirty. His shirt
was disheveled. He looked like he had just gone a few rounds
with Mike Tyson.

"Thanks, Billy."

Cotter managed to sweet talk the owner of the used
bookstore into letting him use the phone. He called the agent
from Homeland Security, drumming his fingers on the counter
as the phone rang. *Voice mail? What the hell?*

"Listen, this is Joe Cotter, A-Team Security. My partner,
Billy . . . well . . . ."

After leaving the message, Cotter limped through the
bookstore, skimming the titles while waiting for a return call.
The bookstore owner was tolerant but watchful.

Cotter halted his pacing. He had a duty to his client, still
unfulfilled. And she had a car.

Turning to the bookstore owner, he said, "I'm sorry. Could I
use your phone again?"

The storeowner set his mouth in a grim line. "If it'll get you
out of here, sure."

After making the call, Cotter bought a book—a well-worn copy of a John le Carré novel—and stationed himself near the nonfunctional phone booth. He must have checked for Liz's car fifty or sixty times before her red Porsche jolted to a halt at the curb.

"What are you waiting for? Get in." Her voice was harsh with anger and hysteria.

The minute Cotter eased into the car, Liz took off like an Indy driver leaving the pits.

"So," she said. "Your man Billy didn't turn out to be the neophyte you thought. What the hell kind of security firm do you work for, anyway?"

Liz continued to rant and Cotter endured the verbal abuse, knowing she was right. A-Team Security wasn't living up to its name when it came to checking out its own employees. Billy was a relatively new hire. He'd only just been assigned to Cotter.

But Billy had fooled them all.

Liz finally stopped her rant long enough to take a breath. Cotter fiddled with his watch and muttered, "Hell, his name probably isn't even Billy."

CHAPTER FORTY-FIVE

JESSICA

I unbuckled the belt, slid it out slowly and held it at arm's length, between finger and thumb.

"Drop it!" Billy said.

I released the belt. It coiled to a heap on the ground.

Where the hell are they? Anyone?

He grabbed my arm and pushed me toward the car.

The last thing I intended to do was get in that car. "Billy, why are you doing this?" I asked, stalling for time.

His face loomed close, his eyes ablaze. "Because some people will pay more for secrets."

My whole body trembled. "Billy, I don't have any secrets."

He lowered his gaze, his lips curled down with disappointment, then raised his eyes to me, fiery with renewed anger.

He aimed the gun and I grabbed his arm, out of instinct, throwing my weight into it and fighting to keep it pointed away.

We kept up a crazy dance for a while, me moving in to try kneeing him in the balls and him stepping back. My laptop and shoulder bag dangled from crisscrossed straps, making it awkward to move.

Finally, I slammed my foot down on his instep. He stopped, wincing. Like a field goal kicker, I swung my foot straight into his groin. As he gasped and doubled over, I thrust my knee up under his chin, snapping his head back. The gun fell from his grasp.

I scrambled for the weapon, as Billy cringed and gulped for air, sprawled on the ground.

Aiming at Billy with quivering hands, I yelled, "I don't know anything! I'm just a student who writes fiction. Do . . . you . . . understand?"

Billy nodded and collapsed onto his back, his arms spread wide in a gesture of surrender. He groaned. "The way you fight, lady, you should work for the CIA."

Done in by stress, I blinked back tears. *Just what I need. A job where I'd do this on a regular basis.*

φφφ

Within a minute, several unmarked cars barreled into view, shuddering to a halt near the house. George exited his car and rushed toward me. "Are you okay?"

"I will be. Someday." I'd dried my eyes and recovered my composure but felt stingy with my words and feelings. I wanted to be left the hell alone.

"In case you hadn't guessed, we lost your signal." George shook his head. "Government issue crap. You'd think after 9/11 . . . ." His voice trailed off.

"How did you find me?"

Cotter appeared, looking a bit worse for wear. "I snuck a tracking device on the car while Billy was running an errand. Never did tell Billy about it. I figured the less he knew, the better. Little did I know. Fortunately, Billy only knocked me out instead of killing me. Guess he didn't want to deal with my corpse in downtown D.C.

"After I came to, I tried to reach the Feds. No dice, but I was able to reach your sister. Billy took my cell phone, but he didn't take this." Cotter pointed to his watch. He hit a button.

"Check it out." The watch face converted into the screen of a mini-GPS tracking device.

"I want one of those." George actually sounded jealous.

I watched men and women in Kevlar vests make their way into the house, guns drawn. "Cynthia. She's hurt," I said.

I tried to explain, but George put a hand on my arm. "They'll see to her. How are you? Did you learn anything?"

"Oh, my God. Yes." I dug the typed Q and A out of the laptop case side pocket and handed it over. George read it with eyes expanding to saucers.

George's female twin appeared at his elbow. George thrust the notes at her. "It's Yellowstone. Alert the federal, state, and local authorities now. We have to stop them before they blow it up."

"You might want this," I said.

They turned to look at the flash drives in my hand.

CHAPTER FORTY-SIX

JESSICA

A flurry of activity followed. Billy was taken into custody. Cops descended on the house, a typical brick rancher. A medic unit arrived at the scene, its two occupants hustling a stretcher and drug box inside. George and his twin took the drives and plugged them into a laptop. From the front seat of their car, the agents were able to connect securely to the Internet with a wireless hotspot device and email the files to their counterparts out West.

George breathed a heavy sigh. "Thank God for wi-fi. It's in their hands now," he said, eyes downcast. He looked up again at me. "We need to debrief you."

Great. Without a word, I opened the car's back door and slid inside. The way I slammed it shut conveyed how I felt.

George's liquid brown eyes gazed at me, warming my insides. "Don't worry. We only have a few questions about what happened."

I nodded. "Can we just be done with this?"

"Soon," he assured me. George gazed toward the house. The EMTs were taking Cynthia out on a stretcher. She wasn't moving.

"What's wrong with her? She was conscious when I left her." I started to scramble from the car, but George placed a hand on my arm.

I ignored the gesture, but he tightened his grip until I thought he'd cut off my circulation.

"Someone gave her a nasty crack on the head," he said. "She may have a serious concussion."

"Could I have hit her that hard?"

George squinted my way. "You hit Cynthia?"

"She asked me to. It was part of my escape plan." I mulled the possibilities. "There was this other man. Never got his name, but he had a deep tan and black eyes. Was he in there?"

George's twin spoke. "Along with our operative, we've found two men dead—one at the door and one in a room. So far."

I really felt like shit. A serious concussion? I slumped back onto the car seat. Could Billy have gotten to her before he appeared at the door? Or the mystery man?

A Kevlar-vested agent emerged from the front door and called, "All clear!"

George lifted a hand in acknowledgment. I wondered what happened to the nameless man with the onyx eyes and weathered brown face.

CHAPTER FORTY-SEVEN

KEVIN

So it had come to this. The group's plans had been revealed and
the secrets were unfolding. Kevin smiled. It felt good to know
he was in control. He held a power no one could thwart.

But the question remained—would the Feds be able to pin
anything on the group?

CHAPTER FORTY-EIGHT

JESSICA

"We've been over and over this," I said. "I don't know his name."

Homeland Security, the FBI, and God-only-knows who else had debriefed me for hours at the FBI headquarters office in D.C. *So much for asking only a few questions.*

I'd been through two books of photos and recognized Lucius, but I didn't see the nameless man with the black holes for eyes.

"Can you describe him?" a ferret-faced man asked.

"Again," I said, pausing for emphasis. "He was reed thin, tall—maybe close to six feet—with tanned skin, wrinkled like he worked outdoors. His eyes were pitch black—beady, ugly."

"The hair. Dark brown? Light?" George asked in a softer voice.

I tried to remember. "I . . . medium brown, maybe? It's hard to recall. The light blinded me. And mainly, I remember those dead black eyes."

"How old would you say he was?" The ferret-faced man continued undaunted.

I shrugged and shook my head. "He could have been an old-looking forty or a young-looking sixty. I don't know. Middle-aged?" Middle-aged men all looked the same to me.

George and Ferret Face seemed to ponder this.

"Whoever he is, we need to find him. How's that sketch coming?" Ferret Face directed the remark to a younger man, who'd worked up a pencil sketch and was clicking modifications into a computer-generated face. Answering questions had distracted me from the fact that he was there.

The artist stopped and showed me the monitor. The rendering wasn't perfect, but it was close.

"His face was thinner around the mouth." I said. "Chin more pointed."

The artist made the changes and showed me again.

"Yes . . . ." I said, the memory blossoming into a clearer image. "I'm starting to remember now."

As the artist put the finishing touches on his rendition, George and Ferret Face conferred with a gray-suited man who exuded the air of a superior. George nodded and murmured in response to what the man said. *What were they discussing?*

The gray-suited man dismissed the two with a curt nod, before striding from the room.

George came over and asked, "How's that sketch coming?"

"I think we may be finished here," the artist said. "What do you think?" He held it up for my inspection.

I looked it over. "That's amazing. It looks almost exactly the way I remember him."

"Good. We need to get that sketch to our people out West." George seemed fidgety, his eyes lit with apparent desire to act.

"So, can I go?" I silently prayed he'd say yes.

"That depends."

What the hell kind of answer is that? I wanted to scream. Instead, I said, "What do you mean?"

"This man?" George pointed to the sketch. "We think he may have returned to Colorado, to try to salvage his operation. Or, at least, destroy evidence of the group's plan."

"Okay," I said. I hadn't a single notion what more I could do to help.

"We need to find this man," George continued. He went on for a bit about the group's operation and the evidence. I was starting to tune out, until he mentioned Fred.

"What about Fred?" I asked.

"The police picked up someone at the airport that the Boulder police suspect in Fred's murder. It's possible that he may be the one who killed Fred. Probably following orders from the unidentified man in charge."

"What makes you say that?"

"The Boulder police also found a gun. Ballistics show it's the one that killed your friend. Now, if we can link the gun to that suspect or this man." He held up the sketch. "Or get a witness, to place him at the scene."

"I can't help you." I thought about the old lady who lived across from Fred. "There is someone who might be able to, though."

"If we can connect one of these men to the gun, that'll connect them with the murder. And your identification would connect the murder to the plan, which takes the crime to a federal level."

Great. I'd gone from spy-in-training to possible witness for the prosecution.

CHAPTER FORTY-NINE

JESSICA

On the plane back home, I buckled into my seat and prepared for takeoff. Saying farewell to Liz had been bittersweet.

"Don't be such a stranger," she'd chided me. "You should visit more often."

"You mean, sometime when I'm not being stalked by wacko extremists?" I'd smiled to show my friendly intentions. "I think I can manage that."

Liz had enveloped me in a hug. Her spicy perfume tickled my nostrils again.

"I love you, you know."

My eyes had filled. "I . . . I love you, too, Liz."

Once we were airborne and settled into cruising altitude, I opened my laptop. I had a big finish in mind for Alexis and Daniel. Not to mention Swede, who'd make another appearance.

I had several hours to kill, so I used the time to bring Alexis back to her sister Katie's condo—with a plan.

φφφ

ALEXIS

The following day, Daniel confronted Mel. "How could you place my fiancé in such a dangerous position? This is my battle to fight."

"I told you this might be necessary," Mel shot back. "As far as the opposition knows, you're dead. We need you to stay that way a little longer."

Alexis spoke up. "He's right, Daniel. If these people get hold of you, they might torture you for the information, whether they get the papers you left for me or not."

Daniel looked into Alexis' eyes. "I wish I'd never done the research. God knows what use it will be put to."

"I won't let the enemy get their hands on your work." Alexis spoke with much more confidence than she felt.

Mel placed a hand on Daniel's shoulder. "Try not to worry. This will be over soon."

Daniel tore his gaze from Alexis and glared at Mel. "Just make sure this lady comes back alive and well."

After a breakfast of buttered toast and strong, black coffee, Mel escorted Alexis to his car and drove her to the front of her sister Katie's condo building.

As Alexis exited the car, Mel called, "Good luck." She closed the door and the car took off.

Katie let Alexis inside the condo, then grabbed her in a bear hug.

"It's okay," Alexis whispered. "We're covered."

Katie nodded. "It's great to see you, sis." The words came out sounding real enough, but forced just the same.

"Well, I guess you know why I'm here."

Katie nodded again and moved stiffly toward a desk in the corner of the room. Pulling a set of keys from her purse, she used one to open the middle drawer and produced another key.

"This opens a safe deposit box at Chemical Bank on Broadway. You'll find what you need there."

"And we're coming with you," a deep voice intoned from the hall.

Alexis glanced toward the sound and a man emerged. She recognized him from the elevator the night she'd arrived. Except for the gun he pointed her way.

"I'll cooperate." Alexis tried to sound genuine. "Just don't shoot me, okay?"

Alexis turned toward the door, with the armed man following close behind. As she opened it, she realized, *He said "we." Who else could he be referring to?*

A strangled cry and sounds of scuffling came from behind her.

Alexis spun around and saw the man with the gun being strangled with a wiry garrote. She blinked, unable to believe her eyes once again.

The man slumped and dropped the gun. Swede let his body fall and picked up the weapon.

Swede glared at Alexis, his lucid green eyes hard as marbles.

On the elevator, Alexis asked Swede, "How did you know I was here?"

"Would you believe a lucky guess?" Swede smiled, but the expression didn't reach his eyes. "Good thing I was there. That guy was up to no good."

"How do you know that?" *And, by the way, didn't you just strangle him?*

"He's one of the people who tried to convince Daniel and me that he was with the Feds. Clearly, he wasn't."

Alexis didn't think anything was clear, anymore. Swede's presence and actions did nothing to allay her fears.

Swede tucked the gun in his waistband. "Next stop, Chemical Bank."

"Right." Alexis wrung her hands. Tension raised her pulse and liquefied her guts.

The elevator doors opened and they stepped into the lobby. The doorman was nowhere to be seen. As they approached the front door, a voice behind them called, "Freeze! Don't move."

Alexis turned and saw Mel aiming a gun at Swede from around a far corner.

Swede quickly drew and fired, but Mel took cover. The shot echoed in Alexis' head. She hit the floor.

Mel reappeared and fired back. Swede took a shot in the leg and went down, screaming.

Swede's gun clattered to the floor. Alexis crawled over and scooped it up.

Mel crossed to Swede and stood over him. "I think your friend will have an interesting story to tell us."

"I don't understand." Alexis said. "I thought the terrorists approached him, too."

"They did," Mel said. "They didn't realize he was working for another faction. One that would pay more for the information."

As a group of officers arrested Swede and called an ambulance, Daniel emerged from Mel's hiding place. He approached Swede and stared down at him.

"You . . . You're supposed to be dead." Swede's astonishment was matched only by his clear disappointment.

"It was you who had me followed that night, wasn't it?" Daniel kept his voice low and even, but Alexis could sense anger beneath the calm.

"You were going to sell our research to the highest bidder," Daniel said. "And you figured you could get your hands on my half of it through Alexis. Am I right?"

"What of it?" Swede's voice dripped disdain. "You're just a goddamned academic. What use would you make of the knowledge?"

Alexis felt a cold ball of fury forming in her belly. *That son of a bitch!*

"I wouldn't give it to people who'd do harm with it." Daniel's voice revealed the depth of his disgust and dismay at Swede's betrayal. "I may be an academic, but at least I'm not a traitor. Or a murderer."

Alexis sprang to her feet and crossed to where Swede lay. She hauled back and kicked him in his leg wound. As the cops dragged her off, Swede's howl could probably be heard all the way to Brooklyn.

Once Daniel had retrieved his portion of the work, the police forced Swede to disclose where he'd put his part of the project. No doubt with promises of a plea bargain, for what they were worth.

Alexis and Daniel later met with Mel at an office in the federal building.

"You done good, kid." Mel smiled at Alexis. "Nice work. Now hand it over."

"What?" Daniel said, clutching the papers.

"You need to give me those papers." Mel's tone was no-nonsense.

"Why? What gives you the right?"

Mel held up his badge. "It's in the interest of national security. You saw what almost happened."

Daniel, who had tensed like a coiled snake, relaxed, but his eyes looked wary.

"The government needs to keep your research in a safe place. One terrorists can't access."

Daniel hesitated before nodding his assent. "I suppose you're right."

He started to hand the papers to Mel. Alexis said, "Wait. What will you do with them?"

Mel shrugged. "That's for others higher up on the food chain to decide."

φφφ

JESSICA

The story was working its way toward resolution. I hoped my own story would also be resolved soon.

CHAPTER FIFTY

JESSICA

The following morning, I reported to the Boulder police station to review a line-up of suspects in Fred's murder. As a uniformed officer escorted George and me to the room, I saw the elderly woman who lived across from Fred's apartment step into the hallway, talking up a storm to the officer with her.

"That was him. I'm positive," she said. "I remember seeing him hanging around outside, waiting. Of course, I didn't think much about it. Plenty of people lurk about . . . ."

Her voice faded as she walked away. I looked at George before we entered the room.

"Well, here goes nothing," I said.

George nodded and opened the door. The room was dark and I could see several men standing in a line through the one-way mirror.

The officer who'd escorted the neighbor returned.

"It's him," I said. "Number Five."

George and the officer looked at each other. I thought George might kick up his heels with joy.

The man identified as Number Five was definitely the beady-eyed Man with No Name.

"All right." George clapped his hands and rubbed them. Even though the Boulder police were handling the murder investigation, George would be able to look over their shoulders since it pertained to national security.

I tried to smile but felt less than enthusiastic.

We sat in a conference room, drinking coffee the color and consistency of burned diesel oil. If I hadn't disliked soda and craved the caffeine, I would've taken a pass. Eight packs of sugar helped a little. Even so, I grimaced with each sip.

A plainclothes detective stuck his head in the door. "We've got a lead on where he may have bought the weapon."

"Assuming he bought it," I said. The two men stared at me.

"Good going," George said. "I'll need a chance to question the suspect. Can you keep me posted?"

"Absolutely. We'll have him ready for you in ten minutes." The detective ducked back out.

"This should be fun," George said. "With a murder charge and other possible federal charges we can bring against this man, we should be able to cut a deal. We're going to nip this group's plans in the bud." He turned to me and added, "You helped make this possible, Jess. I can't thank you enough. Your country owes you a debt."

CHAPTER FIFTY-ONE

SIX MONTHS LATER

JESSICA

Boulder was ablaze with the golden leaves of aspen trees. The air was crisp and cool, but the sun was shining.

Shelley saw me in her office. I took a seat and awaited her verdict.

"I'm still not comfortable with the end," she said.

I can't say I was surprised. Even so, I asked, "Why?"

"I don't know," she said. "Don't you think it's a bit corny? Derivative?"

"Maybe. But I can't picture it ending any other way."

Shelley shook her head and set her tortoise-rimmed glasses aside. "Can you take one more crack at it? Try for a more definite ending. More positive, maybe?"

I realized what she was getting at. "You think I sound like a crack-pot, right?"

She smiled and waved a dismissive hand, though her eyes didn't reflect her casual air.

"You've been through quite the wringer," she said. "You have every right to end this as you see fit. Just be forewarned, others may not like it."

"I know. I'm just writing it as I see it. Anything else would be dishonest."

She handed me her comments. "Good luck. I look forward to seeing it later."

I thanked her and took the comments. Then I returned to my condo and took another look at the ending.

φφφ

ALEXIS

Afterward, as they left the building, Daniel said, "Thank God that's over. Now, we can have a proper reunion."

He placed his arm around Alexis' shoulders and they strolled like any other couple. Almost. Alexis was still very worried.

"What do you think they're going to do with your research?" she asked.

Daniel heaved a sigh. "Probably nothing good."

Mel delivered the research to an intelligence agent, who took the papers to a warehouse in northern Virginia outside Washington, D.C. There, a CIA clerk stowed them in a room filled with file cabinets. Each cabinet held documents deemed sensitive enough to be classified higher than "Top Secret." The file was given a code name, allowing access only to the highest defense department and intelligence community officials. The clerk made sure to enter the name into a ledger: "The Planck Factor Research."

φφφ

JESSICA

As I read the ending again, I tried to imagine how I'd change it. A key rattled in the lock and Joel (the George Clooney look-alike, whose real name I finally knew) came in.

"How's it going?" he asked.

"Great. I've finished a second draft. Now, I just have to revise it a few hundred more times and it'll be ready."

Joel came over and kissed me. I still thought of him as George and still thought he resembled his namesake.

"What was that for?" I asked.

"I need a reason to kiss my girlfriend?"

I grinned. "Of course not."

"If not for you, I wouldn't have transferred to the Denver office."

I nodded. "I'm glad you did."

"I'm so proud you finished the book. That's major. Do you know how many people would like to do that? You have real talent."

My face warmed. "Thanks. I hope I find an agent who agrees with you."

We fell silent. "You never found that man who led the group, did you?" I said.

Joel frowned. "No. But I promise, we're still looking."

"I don't suppose they're any closer to figuring out who actually killed Fred."

"No." He paused and added, "I'm sorry."

It figured. The anonymous killer was probably gone by now. Hiding in a non-extradition country, no doubt.

Even so, I was able to stop his insane plot to detonate Yellowstone. The entire incident still seemed like a bad dream.

"I wonder what happened to their leader," I mused.

"I don't know, but I wouldn't worry, if I were you."

"Sure," I said. Still I had to wonder what he wasn't telling me.

EPILOGUE

KEVIN

Kevin surveyed what he'd written with amazement. As a
scientist and truth seeker at heart, he'd never thought of writing
up his findings in any form except the straightforward scientific
reports he was used to creating. Unfortunately, since it was clear
that the truth was worse than anyone could bear, it had to be
told as fiction.

It was Kevin who'd discovered the terrible possibilities
suggested by the challenge to Einstein's theory. He pondered
the irony of his colleagues' refusal to acknowledge the truth.
The fact that they had dismissed Kevin's concerns as the ravings
of a lunatic had done nothing to minimize the government's
attention to his work.

Thus, by fictionalizing those concerns, he'd managed to
bring them to light in a way that didn't name names or threaten
anyone.

Embedding the truth within yet another story (which,
perhaps not so oddly, also reflected aspects of Kevin's own life)
was a clever way to create even more distance between readers
and the truth, making the dreadful scenario of enhanced atom

bombs and the greater potential for nuclear annihilation that much less real and more palatable.

And making the main characters women took him out of the picture entirely.

He felt incredibly grateful to the doctors who allowed him to use the laptop so he could write for "therapeutic purposes."

Now that the story was finished, Kevin could copy the entire manuscript onto the flash drive he had received in secret from his daughter. He kept it stashed safely under the loose section of floor molding he'd discovered until she could pick it up during her next visit. Thank God for Denise, he thought. His lifeline to the outside world. She'd make sure the book got published. His late wife would have been so proud. He still felt the overwhelming grief of her loss, but reveled in the notion of her living on in his story.

Kevin had paid the highest price possible for finding the truth. He refused to let it lie without trying to get the story published somehow. Perhaps the true story told within a fictional one would lead people to wonder and ask questions.

He read the final chapters over once more, then stared at the pale green walls of his room. Institutional green, people called it. Appropriate. The day was cloudy and milky, thin light seeped through the lone barred window.

The door opened and a young orderly dressed in white stepped inside. He held a syringe.

"Time for your meds, doc."

"I'm just finishing something up," he said, turning back to the keyboard. "Can you continue your rounds and come back?"

The orderly glanced at his watch. "Well . . . .

"Please?"

The young man smiled and shrugged. "Okay. Be back in ten, doc."

After the door closed, he muttered, "That'll be more than enough time, thanks."

Before the orderly returned to give him the shot that would keep him dazed for God-only-knew how long, he typed two more words before saving his work for the last time.

THE END

ACKNOWLEDGMENTS

This book has been a long time in the making. It's been run past a phalanx of discerning readers who have been instrumental in making it the story it is. I would like to thank everyone in my writer's group (past and present) who has had the opportunity to review my drafts and provide their helpful insights, including Shaun Bevins, Ray Flynt, Lynda Hill, Mary Ellen Hughes, Becky Hutchison, Trish Marshall, Sherriel Mattingly, Bonnie Settle, and Marcia Talley. I owe a debt of gratitude to Dr. Alan Linde, Staff Scientist Emeritus at the Carnegie Institution of Washington, Washington, DC, for taking the time to inform me about some of the geological science addressed in the book. If there are factual errors, the fault lies entirely with me. The science may be exaggerated ever so slightly in the interest of creating a more suspenseful story. But you can blame me for that, too.

I'm also deeply indebted to the editor John Barclay-Morton, who also provided insights with respect to the theory of physics at the heart of the story. His comments added dimension to the plot that I hadn't foreseen until he provided me with the edited manuscript. As always, I'm grateful to copyeditor Laurie Cullen for polishing the story. My graphic artist Stephen A. Williams designed an absolutely gorgeous cover. My thanks again to all of these people.

Last, but hardly least, I'd like to thank my brother (a scientist, who took the time to read the book and give it a thumbs up) and sister (one of my most discerning readers). Not to mention my long-suffering husband, Rick, who is always behind me one hundred and ten percent. You are all the best ever.

ABOUT THE AUTHOR

Debbi Mack is the New York Times bestselling author of the
Sam McRae mystery series and a young adult novel, *Invisible Me*.
She's also had several short stories published in various
anthologies and been nominated for a Derringer Award.

A former attorney, Debbi has also worked as a journalist,
reference librarian, and freelance writer/researcher. Along with
writing fiction, Debbi has branched into screenwriting and
podcasting. Her biggest aspirations are to write her memoirs and
make a documentary.

www.debbimack.com